# We Happy Few

## by Rolando Hinojosa

## THE KLAIL CITY DEATH TRIP SERIES

Arte Público Press
Houston, Texas

This volume is funded in part by grants from the City of Houston through The Cultural Arts Council of Houston/Harris County and by the Exemplar Program, a program of Americans for the Arts in Collaboration with the LarsonAllen Public Services Group, funded by the Ford Foundation.

*Recovering the past, creating the future*

Arte Público Press
University of Houston
452 Cullen Performance Hall
Houston, Texas 77204-2004

Cover design by James Brisson
Cover art "Infestation: Títeres Políticos" by José Esquivel

Hinojosa, Rolando.
    We Happy Few / Rolando Hinojosa.
       p.  cm. — (Klail City Death Trip Series)
    ISBN-10: 1-55885-358-8 (trade pbk. : alk. paper)
    ISBN-13: 978-1-55885-358-4
    1. Mexican Americans—Fiction. 2. Rio Grande Valley—
Fiction. 3. College stories. I. Title.
    PS3558.I545W4   2006
    813'.54—dc22                       2005054513
                                              CIP

6 7 8 9 0 1 2 3 4 5          10 9 8 7 6 5 4 3 2 1

Scene: Belken State University
Belken County, Texas

Time: No time like the present

This is a work of fiction; there is, then, no use searching for clues as if this were a roman à clef.

The grotesques that appear here are not the doubles of anyone dead, alive, or known to this writer; the action is likewise imaginary.

# THE DEAN
## I

The head painter stepped back to admire his work while the assistant removed the canvas from the floor, picked up his paint cans and brushes, and placed them in the hallway next to a bench where a student sat reading a fat book.

"Waiting for the prof, are you?"

The youngster looked up and shook his head. "I sit here because all I have to do is go down the stairwell and walk straight into the classroom."

"Pretty smart, sonny. This is Doctor Chalmers' office, know him?"

The student continued reading and shook his head again.

"And you may not, he's to vacate at the end of the term. We painted half of the office and we'll do the rest later when he leaves in a month or so."

Turning to his helper, he said, "You missed a spot there, Charlie. Clean it up. And what you reading there?"

The student shrugged and showed him the book: *Great Expectations.*

"Mostly about dreams, filled and unfilled, retribution, justice, memories, remembrances. . ."

"Wow. Too deep for me, kid. Ready, Charlie?"

He then nodded at the youngster, mumbled inaudibly to his assistant as they headed for the elevator.

Two hours earlier, Elliott Chalmers had received a call from Associate Dean Blanche Weatherall that Dean Brothers wanted to see him. Unable to keep a secret—and for the glory of momentary awe—she added that the Dean had a nice surprise for him. Would eleven o'clock be okay? If not, he, Dr. Chalmers, could choose the hour.

For his part, Elliott—mind in a bit of a whirl, wondering what the nice surprise would be—said that yes, eleven would be fine. Dean Weatherall said she would brew a special pot of coffee for him.

A nice surprise . . . the previous month, on the 22nd of December, he remembered well, the English Department had voted 7 2 1 against forwarding to the College of Liberal Arts' Promotion and Tenure Committee his application for consideration to Associate Professor, and accordingly, as was the custom at Belken State, tenure. That magic word. He knew who the two who voted for him were: Mark Levy, Restoration Drama, and Naomi Sorensen, a Miltonist as was Elliott. The abstention?

Abraham Lincoln Bennett, who else? Good old Abe, noncommital to the last, and here he was a year into his third decade at Belken State and approaching retirement. A retirement which would be followed by a sigh of relief from the two Shakespeare specialists. But, they were willing to hold and suspend their belief until after the farewell party. The gift—God and the Chairman alone knew what that would be—and the hearty congratulations led by the Shakespeare specialists: Tom Morgan and William—not Will, and never Bill, just plain William—Chadwick.

Elliott moved some of his book-packed boxes to make room for the painters. He then partly opened the window; the master painter had said they were applying quick-dry paint, and he could move in anytime after lunch.

Five minutes later, his phone rang. He took off his glasses and placed them in his Out basket as the phone rang again. His answering machine picked up the message. "Elly? This is Mark. Could we have some coffee after your three o'clock? See you."

Glancing at the machine briefly, he dialed Mark Levy's number. "Hello."

"It's me, Mark. Coffee's fine. How're you doing?"

"Ted's assigned me to head the Guest Lecturers Committee. Want to be on it?"

Elliott grinned and said he'd be happy to. "By the way, the Committee on Committees usually selects who's to serve, what's up?"

"Ted owes me a couple. See you at three."

"Right."

The Guest Lecturers Committee. A soft appointment, but something else to be listed on one's Annual Report. Two more committees coming up, but that seventh year, the year of grace. . . He stopped thinking for a second; pursing his lips, he said to himself he would be damned if he put in for consideration again. He'd use the year to expand the article on the *Areopagitica* to a full-blown ninety-page monograph, loaf some and read some and work on that third book. That, he said to himself, was my year, not the university's.

Ten forty-five. Although the walk to the Dean's office was but five minutes away, there was usually someone he'd run into and delay the walk. The green expanse on the Quad was full of students chatting, reading, taking in the sun, and the usual hacky-sack players dodging the Frisbees amid the occasional yell of "You blow away that Calc. class, Joe Bob?" or the more common, "Conjugate and decline this, my man."

Life on the Quad.

Not the best not the worst of students. Well-mannered with their usual "sir" or "ma'm" after each sentence, and most of them working twenty, some thirty hours, a week. Someone had termed it a fourth-rate school but his Dean had said, "Second-rate," knowing some of the liberal arts students could compete with anyone, anywhere. . . Not many, but not a few, either. Engineering? Business? Education? The sciences? All accredited.

His dean, Dean Brothers, had fought hard for Liberal Arts. Most were first-generation college students, and their parents wanted them to go into the professional schools, law, for one, and medicine, for another.

Fine. But the first two years belonged to Liberal Arts. The

Dean here: "We'll teach them to read, to write, and to think." To think critically would come later. It didn't matter, but thinking was called for, and his college was responsible. And yes, he had fought for Lib Arts, and at the state level, too. (Although administration did not want their deans to talk to the state reps and senators.) Nevertheless, he managed to reduce the teaching load from four classes per term to four and three and, finally to three and three.

No, this wasn't the monster in Central Texas, but he had Ph.D.s who wanted to publish, who'd earned their terminal degrees, and he would give them the chance to publish, to carry on research.

Elliott knew this and wondered what the Dean would want with *him*? They'd not met, although Elliott had seen him around campus and at a college reception five, six years ago. John Brooks, a biologist, said, "He's a hard nose." And Elliott, nodding, had reserved judgment, but coming from Brooks, that was a compliment.

At five of eleven, Elliott Chalmers decided to take the three flights of stairs to the Dean's office. To the left of the third floor, mahogany plaques with the bronze-engraved names of professors in the College of Liberal Arts and the prizes and honors won for teaching, service, and for prestigious publications. Elliott observed that the plaques numbered seventeen, some dating back twenty years; completing the set were nine from the past eleven years. The sign to the Dean's office, ENTER WITHOUT KNOCKING, was in bold print on a glass door. Elliott entered the office and was greeted with smiles from three college secretaries. Yes, coffee would be nice, thank you. And the Dean was running a tad late, but he'd left a request that Doctor Chalmers could wait in his office. Would Dr. Chalmers take sugar with his coffee? Cream? An oatmeal cookie, perhaps? Thank you. Yes, right away, and Darla Dalrymple held the door open for Dr. Chalmers.

The word Spartan came to mind when Elliott took in the room. A globe in black, three medium-sized bookcases, two easy chairs, and a two-seat sofa some twenty feet away from the Dean's desk completed the furnishings. The desk was no different from Elliott's except that it was a foot longer and a foot wider. Clean top, too. No phone was visible nor was there an answering machine in sight.

He turned toward a slight noise behind him. Mrs. Dalrymple and the coffee, black and no cream or sugar. And no cookie either. A "Here you are," and the smile never left her face. "Bye, now."

And the coffee was good. Not china, a mug, and the initials of Belken State University, below which showed a book and a lamp embossed in gold plate. As he drained the cup, a medium-sized man, his hair blondish going gray and cut short, entered from an adjoining room.

Elliott rose and waited.

The voice, not unfriendly but caught unawares, said, "Good morning, and who are you?"

"Good morning, Dean, I'm Elliott Chalmers."

"Have a seat, won't you? Some more coffee? Yes? No? Fine. I'll be right back." He picked up some papers from his In basket and walked through a door at the opposite side of the room, next to the smallish sofa. Turning to his left, he said, "This won't take a minute. Go on, take a seat."

●

"Blanche, how are you and who's that professor, I suppose that's what he is, and what's he doing in my office?"

"I called Dr. Chalmers, as you said I hope it was okay for him to wait in your office."

"Oh, yes."

With this, Dean Brothers couldn't stop himself from smiling broadly.

"Sir?"

"Not my Chalmers, Blanche," and with this he laughed, smiling the while.

Before the surprised Blanche Weatherall said a word, the Dean said, "Have Shirley bring me some coffee, oh, and a refill for Dr. Chalmers."

"Oh, God."

"Blanche," kindly.

"Yes, sir?"

"What department?"

He waited as the rattled Associate Dean looked it up. "English."

He smiled at his Associate Dean and returned to his office in fine humor. Blanche Weatherall, after all these years. . .; eleven, was it? Blanche was guilty of a gaffe.

Stepping into his office with a warm smile, he said, "Well, now, what can I do for you?"

Elliott looked at the floor for a moment.

"I really don't know. Dean Weatherall called me to come and

see you at eleven." Elliott made no mention of Dean Weatherall's nice surprise.

"And your name is Elliott Chalmers of the English department. Are you, by any chance, acquainted with Percy Chalmers over in History?"

"I know of him, of course. Two Pulitzers, right?"

Dean Brothers nodded as he sipped his coffee. A slight cough and then, "I've raised one-hundred-thousand dollars since last spring, would have taken me longer except that Mrs. Gloria Goldston died and left the college—not the university—the college—seventy-five thousand dollars toward a chair or a professorship, either one. Belken has a few, but most usually go to Business and Engineering."

Elliott nodded and waited. So that was the nice surprise. Good for that old man.

"Been with us long?"

Elliott replied that this spring term marked the end of his sixth year.

Puzzled somewhat, he told Elliott he didn't remember his name being on the list of associate professor candidates for consideration by the P and T Committee. For his part, Elliott, not knowing what to do with his empty coffee mug, said, "I didn't make it out of the department by a vote of the Budget Council."

The Dean asked for the vote. "7-2-1," said Elliott.

The Dean smiled.

"And the absention, Abraham Lincoln Bennett, by any chance?" Oh, yes, and the Dean laughed as Elliott smiled, despite himself.

Abe, the Dean said, had made no commitment one way or the other for years. Decisive when it came to merit raises, oh yes, but a definite abstainer in promotions. He hated the brother-in-law letters from other universities, faculty referees, and from old friends or members of the committee or "damfool" letters tearing down a colleague who knew more than the letter writer about current scholarship.

"Politics," was Professor Bennett's pronouncement. And he

should have known. He was held as an effective scholar, colleague, and classroom professor by old enemies now retired, by others dead in body and soul for years, and whose lectures in old, brittle, yeller notes were a fire hazard.

Silence followed, not awkward, merely empty.

The silence was broken by the Dean.

His teaching? Above average, for Elliott loved the classroom. Service? Oh yes, the life and soul of university work. The Dean listened carefully.

And then, the inevitable: publications? Well, yes, a book on Milton published by Princeton. Princeton University Press? Yessir. And articles, refereed to death, no doubt. That was better, much better. The old racist joke: "And what have you done to me lately, Ginsberg?" came to mind. Brothers, though, was no racist; insensitive to some issues, yes, but racism was not one of them.

Interested now, he said, "Very nice."

Working on something else at this time? The answer struck Kit Brothers like a rabbit punch. Yes, Elliott Chalmers had signed and mailed back a contract to Rutgers University Press for the manuscript they'd been considering for the past fourteen months.

And was the Budget Council aware of this? A nod.

Well, Jesus Christ, he thought, but did not say. Jesuit-trained as an undergraduate at a small college in Alabama—of all places—he had been trained well. He thought on little Spring Hill and how Wisconsin had replied accepting him within a few weeks of receiving his application toward his graduate degree.

"A Miltonist, then?"

Elliott confirmed this with another nod; looking up at the university-issued clock on the wall, he noticed he'd been talking with the Dean for less than five minutes.

No, he'd made no plans so far. He'd been given the seventh year—much like a governor's reprieve to a death house inmate. The rejection was three and a half months old and no, no plans. As yet, he said rather unconcernedly.

"I'm going to make a call," the Dean said.

K it Brothers picked up the phone, dialed nine, and cupped the mouthpiece: "He's an old friend—we go hunting together in West Texas."

He dialed Stan Weintraub direct; if he's there, Brothers told himself, he'll pick up at the third ring. There.

Stan, my oldest friend, your old hunting buddy.

. . . . . . . . .

Yes, I do, a small favor, but it's customary to ask how I'm doing.

. . . . . . . . .

Well, son, I'm going to make your day.

. . . . . . . . . .

He looked at Elliott and signaled if he wanted more coffee. A shake of the head.

. . . . . . . . . .

Just listen, Stanley. Settle down.

. . . . . . . . . .

Settle down is not a code word. Do settle down. Ready?

. . . . . . . . . .

Sitting down, are you? Well, it's payback time.

. . . . . . . . . .

What do you mean, what do I mean? Was that a groan? Now what kind of attitude is that?

. . . . . . . . . .

Well, that's worth a laugh. Listen. I've a Miltonist in my office.

. . . . . . . . . .

A man whose specialty is John Milton, an Englishman of letters. You social scientists should read more, you know?

. . . . . . . . . .

Now what kind of language is that?

..........

Am I calling at a bad time?

..........

Thank you. It's about justice enveloped in irony. How do you like that? No, no, don't interrupt.

..........

Thank you. I want you to hire him.

..........

Hire, Stan. For the English department. How many Miltonists do you have over there?

..........

You'll be rewarding the Chairman with an unencumbered line.

..........

Of course, it's a bribe.

..........

And don't say you haven't the money.

..........

People have gone to hell nose first for that, Stan.

..........

I'm getting off the line now. His name is Elliott Chalmers, and he's—looking at Elliott—ah, thirty-four years old. You'll receive his vita in an hour. We'll talk tonight about Nick Crowder.

..........

Say again? Oh. Two books: one published, one under contract. First-class schools.

..........

Good man.

He handed Elliott the phone. "I'll be in Dean Weatherall's office."

Two hours prior to his scheduled meeting with Percy Chalmers, Brothers sat in his small, book-laden private office drinking coffee with Bruce Kyle, head of History; they talked on Percival Chalmers' professorship. This done, he told Kyle of an offer he'd received from St. Andrew's College to apply for the Presidency.

His and Kyle's friendship had had a rocky start: Kyle's then wife wanted him to apply for the Deanship at Belken State. He had done so unwillingly and was relieved when the Search Committee did not go for any of the in-house candidates. Instead, it chose an outsider, Kit Brothers, a professor of German at Richland University.

Kyle's wife divorced him soon after and applied for a divorce on Texas's rather liberal divorce laws: incompatability. Their seven-year childless marriage ended quietly.

Kit Brothers stretched and asked, "What do you think, Bruce?"

Kyle, with no hesitation, said, "It's worth considering. You've Fred Winfield on St. Andrew's Search Committee, for one, you're familiar with the place and the people, and the school's philosophy for another, and Nick will champion the cause, I'm sure. The Flads County line is an hour away; you'll have a house, a car, prestige, discretionary funds. . ."

"But?"

"But nothing. It's a hell of an offer and something to think on. Hard."

"Well, I could submit your name, you know."

Bruce Kyle's laugh expressed mock horror. "You can forget that. I built this department, and I'm not going to let it go."

"Look, I've got to go to the library; I've a lunch date with Percy at one-thirty. Let's get together this weekend. Ronnie Guerra wants us to go fourths on a hunting trailer. We can probably go fifths if Jehú or his cousin Rafe wants in."

Kyle gave a thumbs-up. "Trailer? Good idea. We can drive all over Brady's ranch next Christmas." He rose from his chair and headed for the door.

"Bruce, I'll write St. Andrew's and say thanks but no thanks."

Smiling, the lanky, sandy-haired Scot said, "You knew that all along, didn't you?"

"No, I didn't. I needed to talk with you. Besides, my ego. . . ."

"What about your ego?"

"It doesn't need the presidency."

Smiling still, Kyle turned around, waved, and stopped, his hand on the doorknob. "Beatriz and I are thinking about supping across the river tonight."

"I need that. I'll talk to Louise. In fact, I'll call her at the hospital or at home, on my way to the library."

"Bye."

•

Brothers gathered some books and smiled. What would the Catholic boy from Starckville, Mississippi, have done twelve years ago if offered St. Andrew's presidency? Then? At age twenty-seven, the year he was selected as Dean at Belken State?

He walked to the library and left messages at home and at the hospital.

His thoughts went back to Spring Hill College. R.O.T.C. Major Gene Cotten. The Jebbies driving him hard. After Latin declensions, German had come easy. His AB in three years. Louise at Mississippi's St. Mary's. Commissioned. Marriage. Four posts in three years with Wisconsin on his mind. The one year in Nam. After the doctorate, Richland University. Happy years. Chair at Richland and then Dean at Belken. His last conversation with VP Doug Thomson: good kids at Belken State, not the best quality. Most are first-generation college students. What that school needs is a strong dean in Liberal Arts and that's you, Kit. The president is a most capable man and he's got a VP for Academic Affairs who runs the place. Much to learn from both. The VP is a Brit Lit man and looks kindly on Liberal Arts. The president, Nick Crowder, is honest, open, and has raised money and standards.

Richland was your first home, wasn't it? You'll do well there. Anyway, they've got a competitive baseball team, and Thomson had smiled. Baseball. Spring Hill. Coach Davey Doyle, who went up for a cup of coffee with the old K.C.A's. Chuck Finley, owner, boss, and slave driver. Him and his designated hitter and those crazy softball-looking uniforms. Davey D. fielded a ton but hit 210 and was sent down. As Mike González said, "Good field, no hit." Davey Doyle, a born teacher. "Get your foot out of the bucket, Brothers. Lean into it, get ahead of the pitch. Use your wrists, Kit. The wrists." Graduation. Louise. Fort McAlester, Alabama, followed by Benning, then Knox, to wind up in Fort Hood, Texas. Great tank trails in that place. First lieutenant. Hueys in Nam with Wisconsin on his mind. Father Francis Xavier at Spring Hill again, Coach Doyle, and Major Cotten. Both dead, these two. Three years at Wisconsin, hungry for the degree. Good years. Louise.

He crossed the busy diagonal that led to the library.

The searching eyes of the sergeant in charge of the Hueys: ". . . but go ahead and take a look, Lieutenant, sir." It was men's lives and his, not the sergeant's, responsibility for tests, checks, inspections, maintenance, information to show if the Hueys were due to be worked on, supplied, and operated. "I take pride in what I do, Lieutenant." Pride . . . pride goeth before a fall.

He walked into his carrel and called his wife again.

He caught himself humming as he packed his valise, an old friend. The secretaries had left, the occasional noise was that of the janitors—not called that anymore. Building something or other. And here came one now—Herlinda who sold tamales at Christmastime. Hello, Doctor. Overworked, underpaid. A Mexican, a Mexican American, but no, not a Hispanic and most certainly not a Chicana. An old term, he'd been told, but no deep roots in the Valley. Good night, sir. And good night to you. Louise had been thrilled at going out to dinner. Tough day at the hospital: two four-year-old twins injured in a wreck. Natal, prenatal, pediatrics, all the same to Louise Brothers, to Louise Larsson (that's two esses, please) Brothers. Home. A glass of wine, tie unloosened, shoes off, sitting quietly, enjoying each other's company as the sun went down. It was May and it was hot and would be for months to come. Little to no shop. That'd be tonight. Peking duck—don Santiago Li, the old Cantonese whose sons and daughters had enrolled their sons and daughters in Catholic schools on the Texas side—across, as the Valleyites say.

*El Submarino Club*, Alfonso Fong, Prop. Yellow paint, years before the Beatles were born. A quiet bar. Old man Fong typing on what must have been the oldest Olivetti anywhere.

The invitation for the Presidency at St. Andrew's. Hmph.

"What's that about?"

"Sorry, Babe."

"Can it wait?"

"Oh, sure."

"I'll be ready in half an hour. And you, you stay and finish that claret."

The duck was superb: crisp and close, but only close, to a slight char; the ginger announced itself when the duck left the kitchen. One waiter carved, one served, and the third kept the Chinese wine chilled to the freezing point. The conversation consisted of smiles, glances, followed by a soft smacking of the lips.

Mr. Li, never one to bother his guests, would stand, lips pursed in a slight grin, and accept the silence as the heartfelt compliment to his wife's and their two sons' cooking and preparation. His almost imperceptible signal brought the table the third and final bottle of wine.

He knew Dean Brothers' predilection for bell peppers; his wife—who, within earshot of Mr. Li—said she'd kill for the snow peas. As for the duck, there had been no hurry in its preparation. Not with those four at the table who always called hours ahead of time. Mr. Li, a first-class chef himself at one time until he lost, he said, his sense of taste, was content seeing the professors and their wives at play—eating and drinking, yes, but at play: relaxed, quiet murmurings, the exchange of glances around the table, signifying that whatever happened at work today, whatever would happen in days to come, those decisions would wait their turn; for now, the meal.

The last bottle, as always half empty, was retired from the table. The foursome walked to the small bar (noiseless, set in the back, where one had to walk through two doors before reaching their favorite nook which held four armchairs). Cointreau followed, and this signaled the conversation, a standard practice.

Bruce Kyle turned to Beatriz and said, "A bit of shop. It's serious, though, and it will have influence on all of us."

Beatriz Guerra asked, "Am I in this?"

"By way of your uncle. After all, he's one of the twelve regents."

Beatriz nodded absently and reached for Kyle's hand.

"I didn't tell you this morning, Kit. It was Percy's day, and I could see no reason to sour his appointment."

Louise looked at her husband who waited expectantly.

Kyle, never one to be brusque or to look for the easy way out, said, rather quietly and as if in pain, "It's Nick. He has prostate cancer... and I think he let it go too long. He's been taking something for it, but don't ask me what."

At this, Louise Brothers reached across the table for a fortune cookie as the table grew quiet. Crowder had been a silver medalist as a youngster representing the United States. And to be brought down by this?

Louise shook her head slightly before speaking. "At the Thanksgiving dinner last term, I thought he'd gained weight during the summer. He looked," and here she paused for a moment. "Well, he reminded me of Pompidou when he was taking medication, steroids perhaps, which caused his face to swell."

"Did you know, Kit?" He looked at Beatriz and shook his head. "No, not a thing."

"Do you think Wild Bill will throw his hat in the ring for the third time?" Louise, having said this, frowned rather sadly.

The table grew quiet again.

Bruce Kyle thought on the Vice President for Administrative Services; not a logical choice, not on Wild Bill McVicar, a hail-fellow-well-met, a teller of jokes, a racist who had no clue he was one. A campus politician and a most able public speaker who knew every regent on a first-name basis.

Ah, thought Kyle, again. But there was the legislature; not well-liked there, and Kyle wondered if Ian Cameron McVicar was aware of that. He had to be, he was no fool. But there was one quarter he'd failed to cultivate: the Mexican American Caucus, and, in particular, the Valley's State Senator, a banty rooster whose son, now at M.I.T. with a healthy scholarship, had failed to be admitted to Belken State's graduate program. Whose fault was that? Not McVicar's, surely, what did he know about admissions? But the History head knew the state senator who'd called him on the phone. His son was a Bachelor of Science graduate in Physics and Math, and he'd applied. Kyle, in his usual straight talk, said the boy was better off at M.I.T. But it rankled, the senator had said. His mother wanted their son here, at home. To her, Massachusetts was in another world.

"Just thought I'd let you know, Bruce." No anger, no resentment. They were friends, friends who had never, in over fifteen years, used one another.

On the way to Li's restaurant, he'd told her of the St. Andrew's offer. Louise knew Kit wouldn't apply for the presidency—pressure from friends or no pressure, she knew.

But there would be pressure for the Belken State presidency. Well-intentioned and all, but pressure. As for Kit, he had said he would want to see an outsider who'd come in, retain some, transfer others, in brief, clean house. An outsider could do it; he or she—what was her name, Louise? could do it. You know her. We met her at the Regional Administrator's Conference in Corpus Christi. . .

"Christine. Christine . . . sorry."

"No, I can't think of her name, either. Dynamic, though."

Louise gathered the cookie crumbs and placed them in an ashtray.

Beatriz Guerra had sat listening, turning from one to the other. She thought on her uncle Lalo. He'd push for a Mexican American—he had not gotten over losing Leo Flores to UC Santa Cruz. He knew there was no comparing the presidency of Belken State to a chancellorship in the UC system, and yes, Nicky Crowder was a fine president, and he had raised not only money, but morale as well. A well-run campus with merit raises where raises *were* merited. A dean or two had gone back to the classroom, he'd done away with the baccalaureate services—no one minded since few attended—and he had appointed a committee which spruced up the graduation exercises, shortening the speeches to give the parents and spouses a tightly run, one-hour-fifteen-minute program where everybody would walk across the stage. It fit Belken, and Crowder had figured that out in his first year: this was a family affair for the graduates and for spouses and parents and relatives who drove across Texas to see one of their own graduate.

His, too, was the open house every other Tuesday for students to vent, and he'd listen. No, there was nothing her uncle didn't know regarding Nick Crowder. And now this, cancer of the prostate and too far gone in Louise's assessment. Her uncle, Lalo, an eleventh-grade dropout who opened a mom-and-pop store to begin with was worth a not-moderate fortune fifteen years later. "A decisive uncle, my Uncle Lalo. He'd walked into the Klail City National Bank and told the first secretary he saw, 'I speak to the President of the bank or no one.'" A rough-and-ready self-made man, incorruptible, Beatriz's uncle. Appointed regent by a Democratic governor and reappointed by a Republican. He knew the game: money to both sides, no partisanship. She knew he wanted a Mexican American, man or woman, but a Mexican American, unless. . . unless there were some intangibles, and he was not intransigent. He'd been burned by two top Mexican American administrators who talked the game, but that was what it had been: talk.

"I think Uncle Lalo, if it comes to this, will fight for a Mexican American president, but it would have to be someone like Leo Flores."

"He should," said Kit Brothers. "It's only logical, too. The times they are a-changing, but in this case, the changes have been a long time in coming. Some progress, sure, but we're a traditional minority school, in the heart of the Valley, and Nick Crowder has done wonders. Sure, some Anglos call us Taco Tech, Tamale U, and some Mexican Americans use the terms, too. We can disregard them; they're a minority, and a damned small one at that.

"As for Lalo Guerra, we know what he wants; he wants Belken to improve and if an Anglo like Nick did it, and another one comes along, fine. I don't think he's wedded to a Mexican American solely on a *raza* quota. And neither is Pete, up in Houston. They want a good school. Trouble is, how many Leo Flores's are out there? For that matter, how many Nick Crowders?"

The waiter waited. That conversation, whatever it was, was serious. He signaled the bartender for a magnum of mineral water.

Looking at all three, Bruce Kyle said quietly, "If I'm selected to the Search Committee, I'll see to it."

Beatriz looked at him and took his hand. "The best, right? The best, whoever and whatever the candidate is."

They all agreed that that was the way it should be, the best. This wasn't the past anymore.

Kit Brothers signed the bill. "It's been," he said, smiling.

"One last thing, though. Remember, eight of the twelve are holdovers, and they voted for Leo, and all twelve voted for Nick. We've a grown-up Board of Regents now."

Louise finished the conversation: "My Dad always said if lawyers could count on anything, it was not to count on the jury."

He awoke with a start and tried to control his breathing. He glanced at Louise breathing comfortably, the soft snore which she denies. He'd been back in Starckville, a Boy Scout, helping in his father's store and gas station.

●

Look at it, Kit. That, son, is one of the many faces of hate, using the Lord's cross as a symbol of hatred. You may know some of those kids. Will Mitchell say they were high schoolers. You're bound to know them, sit in the same classroom, play ball with 'em. A hateful thing that cross, black as the colored folk they hate.

Hate and fear, Kit. Mayor Ramsey stopped gassing here, when I took Wallace Brown on as an attendant. Worse, when you took over, I placed Wallace in as sack boy and he brought over his cousin, Tinsley Meacham. Some, later many, and finally none shopped at the store, except for the passersby. Four months. Didn't bother going to the bank for a loan. Your mom and I scrimped and saved and we kept going. No church parish then; a mission, and the priest came and went, marrying and burying, baptizing and christening, first communion, all the sacraments, Kit. But he never asked about the store. The Lord saw that we got a new bishop. That priest was replaced. The new one, a recovered alcoholic from the Confraternity of St. Paul, a C.S.P.; Can't Stop Preaching, he used to say. Straighter than any arrow made by man.

Hellfire and brimstone, son. So you stop buying groceries and your gas at Mr. Brothers' place, eh? Well, dear people, he is named most aptly. He *is* a Brother. And some walked out. A few came back, and he harped on and on: Dear parishioners, although he doesn't, Mr. Brothers could say with Job, "All my inward friends abhorred me, and they whom I loved are turned against me."

And those who returned talked about nothing but your baseball. They talked of Ole Miss, Mississippi State, 'Bama. Ha! Them baseball scouts—cross burners, your mother and I called them. Probably were, and your mom wrote a letter to Spring Hill. 'Bama, was it? Well, that's where you went, Spring Hill, Alabama, all right.

Your uncle helped. No, not with money. What money is a Jesuit gonna have, anyway? Your grades and your goodness, don't be ashamed, Kit—and the baseball helped. And you worked for that athletic department, and at the library, wherever there was work.

Graduation. Jesus God Almighty, a scholarship to Spring Hill, Kit. The only thing you'd let us buy was the sport jacket. Your uncle Henry was right: "What that boy can't do, I don't know. He's got a future and a good head to go with it."

But it was that cross, wasn't it? You didn't say a word when we came from Black Town. You were angrier than I've ever seen you, and I was afraid, scared of what you'd do in school. But you beat 'em: best grades, best hitter and fielder, and those three two-hundred-dollar scholarships to go anywhere. You thanked the people personally in their homes and then placed the money in the bank and worked at Mayor Ramsey's hardware until a week before you left for Spring Hill.

You sent happy letters. Got yourself a girl and sent us pictures. A strange name, Larsson, but what a girl she was. Your mom loved her to death. A nurse, is what she wanted to be. The nuns enticed her, but she wanted to work with babies, even before they were born. And she did: a B.S. and an R.N., I was lucky to have your mom pick me. I didn't much like books, but I could work, and I decided I'd work for no man. Your mom taught at the Beale Elementary and she taught the colored youngsters at home.

Died at age forty-two, Kit, and I asked you to speak at her funeral. And Louise and I cried and were proud of it.

But it was that awful black patch of a cross. You couldn't live in Starckville, Mississippi, after that. Why did we come here? Ha! For a Catholic city, New Orleans also hated Catholics, Italians, mostly. Lynched some 'em, and burned 'em, too. Up they moved to Shelby and some to Starckville. The Corelli family was the feistiest, and my daddy's first store was in Little Italy.

Yeah. . . they always give titles to people and places. You and I know every name they fixed on the coloreds. Lord, how they dreamt 'em up. And I was scared, scared of what you would say, would do. But you took it, lost some so-called friends, and we knew, your mom and I.

Everett, that boy could take on everyone of those—and God knows I want to swear, but I won't call 'em what they are—*haters*, haters was her strongest word.

Spring Hill. And then, in your junior year: forty dollars a month from R.O.T.C. and you sent some home, and we sent it right back. You'd earned it, Kit.

I was against the war, and so were you, but you took the oath, and that was that. Vietnam. Then on to Wisconsin, you and Louise into the bargain, and her on partial scholarship.

No, no future here, no, not in Starckville, son.

# THE STUDENTS
## II

Darla Dalrymple, the senior secretary, was chatting with Dean Blanche Weatherall, when the student Eric Rodríguez walked into the Dean's front office. They saw a grim-faced, green-eyed young man in a state of agitation.

"May I help you?"

"My name is Eric Rodríguez. I'm a sophomore in Sociology, and I want to see the Dean." He looked around nervously and said nothing more.

"Have a seat, won't you? I'll see if the Dean's available."

"You tell him I want to see him. I want to see him now."

Slightly startled but composed, Darla Dalrymple said, "I'll ask him."

At this point, Dean Weatherall left the door to her private office open and went to see Dean Brothers as three more students joined Eric Rodríguez and stood, arms crossed, next to him.

Dean Weatherall briefly explained the student's request as the intercom came on: "Dean Brothers."

Looking up from a letter of recommendation he was writing for Elliott Chalmers, he asked, "Yes, Darla. What is it?"

"Four students (Brothers looked at Blanche Weatherall who expressed surprise) wish to see you."

"Did they say what it was about?"

"No, sir."

Blanche Weatherall said, "The kid looks edgy—nerves, I think."

"Tell 'em to come in."

Eric Rodríguez stood five-foot-nine in his high-heeled Ortiz custom-made cowboy boots. The Dean guessed his weight at 150 pounds or less. The boots were set off by a light-gray *guayabera* shirt and dark-gray Wrangler denims.

"Hello, I'm Dean Brothers."

"Sir, we are going to occupy Old Main and stage a sit-in."

A sit-in. Kit Brothers hadn't heard or used that term in over thirty years, not since Vietnam and Mario Savio's rallies at Cal, not since the deaths of Bobby Kennedy and Martin Luther King. Not since. . .

"And I want you to know we're not going to back down until we get what we want, sir."

"You came to see me. Obviously you think I can help. If so, in what way?"

"I, and my committee, went to see Dean Borchers at Business, but he wasn't in. Dean Coryell wasn't in either, nor Dean Esparza in Education."

Ah, the Court of Last Resort: the College of Liberal Arts. "I see."

"Sir, we want you to know that Chicano students on this campus face institutionalized racism on a daily basis. We won't stand for it and we want changes in attitudes. Those are our demands and issues, racism and attitudes."

Institutionalized racism. Who had the kid been reading? Well, at least young Rodríguez hadn't used viable, nonnegotiable demands and harassment. Buzzwords that disappeared by the late seventies.

"Won't you sit down?"

"Sir?"

"All of you, sit down. Let's talk."

The youngsters hesitated for a moment, looked around for chairs and went to them.

"Racism, you said. Were you, or was a member of the committee or students you represent, victims of racism? Did they give you the names of a professor or professors and examples?"

"No names, no, sir. They're afraid of reprisals. . ."

Reprisals, I'd almost forgotten that one.

"Let's see, Mr. Rodríguez. Belken State has a student population of 14,740. Twelve-thousand nine-hundred are undergraduates. Of close to the 13,000 undergraduates, there is a 1,700 Anglo enrollment. That leaves 1,040, more or less, who are M.A. candidates, counting the four Blacks enrolled here."

"Yes, sir?"

"Do you and the committee represent the Chicano students and only the Chicano students?"

"No. We represent all Hispanics."

"Good. Why don't we hold an open forum at the Lucy Ramírez Auditorium, early next week, before finals. Pass the word, publicize it in *The Belken Bee*, and we'll go from there."

"That sounds like a delaying tactic. Besides some of us have jobs, sir."

"The great majority of our students work, Mr. Rodríguez. You're an adult, a taxpayer, old enough to serve and die for your country, to marry, and everything else that responsible adults do as a matter of course. You have taken the responsibility to make a charge and a complaint, a complaint that is within your rights as a citizen and as a student. Why not talk to the committee?"

"Thank you for your advice, but we're taking over Old Main, and you can't stop us."

"You won't consider the suggestion of a meeting at the auditorium?"

"No, that's why I came to see you."

"You're not asking me permission to have your sit-in in the Ad building, are you? And don't forget, some classes meet there. We can't have a disruption of classes, at any time, by any one, without consequences to those responsible."

"We've, ah, we've considered that aspect, sir."

"By the way, have you read Lenin?"

"Lenin? No, sir, he's a Communist."

"The founder of modern communism and one-time leader of

the early Union of Soviet Socialist Republics. You're right, he was a Communist. He also asked the following questions at every meeting: 'What needs to be done?' and 'What are we to do?'"

"Sir?"

"Whatever answer was given him, it didn't matter. It was to be his way or else."

"But what does this. . .?"

"Excuse me for a moment. I have the duty and the responsibility to notify the President of your intentions and will do so now while you are here or shortly after you leave. To do otherwise would constitute a violation of my duties and responsibilities as an officer of the university. What the President's decision will be, I have no idea."

Eric Rodríguez rose from his chair. "Well, thank you, *sir!*"

"There is such a thing known as insolence through manner. That aside, your decision not to consider an open forum at the auditorium will be noted. And note this as well: if you were an Anglo, a true minority at this institution, who lodged a complaint against one or several of the ninety-plus Mexican American faculty who used or made personal racist remarks, we would act in the same way.

"These are the nineties, Mr. Rodríguez, and in Belken County and at Belken State, you are not a minority."

"But we are a minority."

"Good day, Mr. Rodríguez."

Eric Rodríguez stopped as he came to the glass door of the outer office. At the same time, Blanche Weatherall was on her way to the bathroom.

"The Dean's a Communist. He reads Lenin!"

"Excuse me, I have some business to attend to."

When President Crowder walked out of his private washroom, he faced four students standing in front of his desk. Mary Díaz, the head of the President's staff, hesitated for a moment and then said, "I'm sorry, Mr. President, they, they just walked right in."

"Thank you, Mary."

Facing the young, defiant faces, Nick Crowder said, "Good morning. What can I do for you?"

Eric stepped up and said, "We're occupying this office. Later on, some committee members of the Chicano Cultural Committee intend to occupy the building. This is a peaceful sit-in."

"And you are?" motioning to Cindy Villarreal.

She introduced herself and pointed to Thelma Lou Cantú and Juan Perez Gómez. "I'm a fifth-year graduating senior, sir. Thelma Lou?"

"I'm a six-year graduating senior."

"Congratulations. That would be at the end of the month or during the summer term?"

The senior girls spoke at once, "On May twenty-second, sir."

"I'm from Klail, sir. Thelma Lou's from Ruffing, and Juan here's from Mexico."

"Mexico? Barrones, Reynosa?"

"Control, Mr. President."

"And you, Mr. Rodríguez?"

"I'm from here, Klail City."

"Well, you better move some of the chairs around. They're a bit heavy, so you help each other out.

"You were saying, Mr. Rodríguez?"

"Yes," almost shouting. "We want to protest and make our nonnegotiable demands."

"You're within your rights, but I've a university to run, and you must excuse me."

Cindy Villarreal stood up. "You're throwing us out?"

"No, that's not my style. Occupy away, but I've some meetings to attend to, and obviously, I wasn't expecting you."

"And?"

"I'll leave the office and the building to you and your committee. Before I do so, however, I wish to make some matters clear.

"Juan, you are a Mexican citizen; you have standing as a student but not as a citizen of this country. You pay Texas tuition rates because of an agreement with Mexico's federal government, and American students enroll in Mexican universities under the same privileges.

"You have, however, no legal rights and, if disruptive, expulsion is a distinct possibility . . . .

"Sit-in, if you will, but (and here Nick Crowder stood up) whatever trash is left in the offices and hallways is your responsibility. I will not have the men and women who clean your dorms, the classrooms, the labs, the offices, the libraries, restrooms, the Student Union, in short, every building on campus and the grounds on which they stand, I will not have them clean up after you. They're overworked, they're people in their fifties and sixties, and they do their jobs daily and nightly so you may enjoy a clean place in which to work.

"As I said, I've meetings to attend. You must excuse me, I have to leave now."

And he did so. Mary Díaz was waiting for him. "The students, sir?"

"Leave them there. What's on for this morning?"

She looked at her appointment book as the President headed for the visitors' lounge to wait for the elevator.

"You have a meeting in, let's see, twenty minutes from now with the Physical and Natural Science deans, faculty, and staff.

"And I've two messages. One from Mrs. Crowder, the second from Dean Brothers. I was coming in to deliver them when the students barged in. Sorry, sir."

"Why the smile, Mary?"

"It's a coffee for you. A party over there and sponge cake, too."

"Sponge cake, ha!"

"And, sir, please accept this, will you?"

"What is it?" Curious and appreciative.

"Open it, sir. It's a medal from all of us. A Catholic medal of St. Rochus. I know you're not Catholic, sir, but. . ."

"It's sweet, Mary, very sweet. Oh, and now I've made you cry."

"Excuse me, sir, I have to go freshen up."

"Bye, Mary." The voice kind, level as always; he looked through the glass doors; the staff stood there, smiling.

Cindy was the first to speak up. Looking at Eric Rodríguez, she said, "Well? What do we do now, Genius?"

"What's wrong with you? We use the phone and we call everybody up, that's what."

"What phone? Besides, the guys are probably in class right now."

"The President's phone, whose else?"

"I don't think you should do that."

"And why not, Miss Villarreal?"

"Listen, you little shit. I'm graduating this month. I've got relatives from Houston, Dallas, and San Antonio coming down to see me on that stage when I get my diploma. That's why!"

"What about our agenda?"

"What agenda? We occupy the building, and then what?"

"Well, Thelma Lou, I thought at least you'd stick with me."

"Shove it, Mister. I've spent six-and-a-half years here. Spent my money, my folks's money, and I've got loans to pay. It's life. You got that?"

"And what about me? You heard him: I'm a Mexican. I've got no standing. I still got three years to go and if I'm kicked out my father will kill me, and if he don't finish the job, my brothers will . . ."

"So? Are all of you going to walk out? What will they say in California, New Mexico, Arizona?"

"I say, screw 'em. They come here, b.s. our law students and us, and then go back. Well, I don't see them getting their shit together. They're always in turmoil."

"Cindy's right. We're Texas, we're from the Valley. We're not sophisticates like them, but we've got more reps in D.C. than they do."

"What are you talking? D.C.? What the hell is that? This campus needs to be cleaned." Eric raised his voice and looked at each individually.

"Cleaned up is right, Eric. Listen, the whole damn time I've been here, I haven't said hello to any of those women who clean up after us. Not one word. Not one. Jesus Christ! They're in their fifties, man. They're proud we're here. And who the hell are we, anyway?"

"We're activists!"

"I'm a jerk for listening to you, Eric. But you're a bigger jerk!"

"Sit on it, Cindy, and you too, Thelma Lou."

"Screw this. I'm going to the dorm and write a letter of apology to the President and a letter of thanks, too."

"Thanks? What the hell for?"

"You're a sophomore, Eric," Cindy Villarreal said. "When I came here, President Crowder had been here some three years. Well, Genius, there were maybe a dozen or fifteen *raza* profs then, tops. Five years later, we have sixty, seventy, maybe eighty, I don't know. You see them all over the place. I've been to gradu-

ations here and no less than thirty of 'em show up. Everytime.
They talk to the folks. How do you like that?"

"And they're proud of us, damn you."

"I see I'm in the wrong crowd here."

Thelma Lou cut in. "And don't call me a *vendida*, you little
shit. You do, and I'll cut it off for you."

"And what about me?"

"Well, what about you, Juan?"

"That letter you're gonna write. Can I sign it?"

"No!"

"No? But . . ."

"The man deserves better than that. You write him personally.
You do that, and he'll appreciate it."

"Quitters, all of you. That's what you are, quitters."

"Raising your voice won't help, Mr. Rodríguez. We've all
been fools, but we were worse fools. To be taken in by someone
who calls Dean Brothers a Communist."

"No, he didn't, Cindy."

"Didn't you hear him? Jesus, Mary, and Joseph. The Dean is
a deacon at St. Cecilia's, for God's sakes. He even gives the hom-
ily sometimes. Takes up the collection plates. He's a member of
the community."

"Really? Well, where were you when all of this was taking
place?"

"Screw you, Eric. My dad runs a dry cleaning place, and his
friends meet there. President Crowder has gone there to talk to him
and to the other parents. He can't offer much money for scholarships, not with UT blowing in here with their deep pockets?"

"Aw, UT doesn't give that much, anyway."

"That's right, Thelma, but they come with their prestige and
with *raza,* whose Spanish belongs in the first grade. My dad says
President Crowder is proud of Belken State. He talks to people, he
raises money, he wears himself out."

"I came here to protest."

"Eric, Belken isn't perfect, but it's home and it's ours."

"What are you, a booster? You want a job here?"

Cindy, "I wouldn't mind."

"Nor I," said Thelma Lou.

"And me?"

"We're leaving, Juan. It's up to you."

"Yeah, it's your office now, Eric."

"Bunch-a shits."

"Ex-shits, Snot Nose."

Thelma Lou stopped at the door and said, "My dad's a meat cutter at H & H. You know how the President introduced himself to my dad? He said, 'Good afternoon, Mr. Cantú. I'm Nick Crowder.' Not Professor Crowder, not Doctor Crowder, not President Crowder, but Nick, Nick Crowder."

"He's a con man. That's just for show, pretending he likes us. Boy, when I think of having you as friends . . ."

Cindy ended it. "You can stop thinking now. Let's go, guys."

Thelma stopped to look in her backpack. She reached into a small zippered pocket and said, "Here's a quarter; buy yourself a clue. And I've got news, too: you're not so hot in bed, either."

A week after Eric Rodríguez had led the march on Dean Brothers' office, Dean Weatherall was checking the College of Liberal Arts' grades for the graduating seniors. The youngster approached Dean Weatherall excused himself, and asked if the Dean were available. If she recognized him, it would have been a miracle. To her, all the students, men and women alike, wore the same uniform: blue jeans, T-shirts, tennis shoes, and, if the women students were going to work after class, makeup, hair brushed, a dress, and high-heeled shoes. Did he have an appointment; he shook his head. With a please wait here, she entered her office first and then crossed it to the Dean's side entrance.

"A student to see you, Dean."

He glanced at his watch; half an hour before his talk with the Spanish section of the Modern Language department. "Show him in."

Eric was wearing glasses instead of his contact lens. The khaki trousers were starched stiff, and his blue, buttoned-down oxford shirt contrasted sharply with the boot-wearing student in a guayabera shirt and denims.

Kit Brothers looked up and pointed to a chair. "Yes?"

"Good morning, Dean. I'm Eric Rodríguez. I was here last Friday. With the students," he added rather shyly.

Kit looked at the youngster and, after a  second or two, recognized him.

"Oh, yes. What can I do for you?"

"Sir, my parents told me to come and apologize and to say I was sorry for my actions of last week."

The Dean nodded and said, "Do sit down."

The youngster sat at the edge of the armchair.

"Is there anything else you wish to add?"

After a slight cough and in a slight, uncomfortable voice, he said, "No, sir."

"Well, I have. Tell your parents I'm happy to accept their apology."

"Beg pardon, sir, I'm the one that's apologizing."

Kit scratched his head and said, "You're an obedient son, I can see that, but you're here because they sent you. You embarrassed them."

"Did you call 'em, sir?" After a pause he said, "Yes, I guess I did."

Kit Brothers pressed on.

"Guessing has nothing to do with it."

Baffled, Eric looked at the floor. "Sir?"

"I was quoting you. You said, 'I guess I did.' You did, they were embarrassed and they did the honorable thing. And I'll tell you why they're not here."

"Sir?"

"Universities, banks, some churches, at times, public buildings like city hall, for instance, their size tends to inhibit some people. The buildings, the crowds, and, on a campus such as this one, the rush and the young age of the students, also shakes 'em up. We're too much for them. Do you see that?"

"I don't think I do."

The Dean pushed his chair away from his desk.

"I'm guessing, but I think you're a first-generation college student."

Eric Rodríguez's eyes opened wider still. He knew the words, but what did they all mean?

"You're the first person in your family to attend a university, am I right? Are there brothers and sisters?"

A shake of the head by the youngster.

"I would like to meet your parents. . . have them come here. After all, some, all, or part of their tax money was spent to build

Belken State, and another part of their money—hard-earned, I expect—made it possible for you to come here."

The words were spoken in Kit Brothers' low, neutral voice and with his usual tone, neither commital nor accusatory, and yet the nineteen-year-old's eyes were glassed over.

"What do your parents do for a living?"

"My folks?. . . My dad works for the city, he's a meter reader and handyman, and my mom makes and sells *coronas*, uh, wreaths for cemeteries. It's hard work."

"I don't doubt it." Small town, university town, Starckville again.

"And I work, Dean. I serve food at The Happy Burger at the Union, fifteen hours a week."

"A hardworking family."

"Ah. . . well, yes, I guess we are."

"There you are, Mr. Rodríguez, guessing again."

The youngster sat back, the tension relaxing, but not entirely comfortable, as if waiting for the other shoe to drop.

"My dad speaks English, and my mom, she speaks it too." Now completely relaxed.

"Cindy Villarreal came to see me two days ago. And then the other girl. . ."

"Thelma Lou, sir."

"Right. She was here yesterday afternoon, after work at the library."

"Oh?"

And now the Dean, as Dean, said, "They came in on their own."

"I'm sorry, sir."

Kit Brothers glanced at his watch: a quarter of an hour. He was not about to let go of the bone yet. . . . "I don't want to know who influenced you, or what led you to invade the President's office the way you did. But, since you're acting as a messenger, I'm going to use you as a messenger."

He let that one sink in.

"Sir?"

"Whoever pushed you into this should apologize to your parents, and I mean now, today, in person, not over the phone and not by letter. I don't care to know who it is, Eric Rodríguez. You caused grief and embarrassment, and perhaps disappointment to two good people who love you and they deserve better.

Without raising his voice, Kit said, "No, don't interrupt. As I said, I'm sure you understood what I said. I also want you to know what I mean. It took a lot of heart to come here, I want you to know that. As did the two young women."

"And Juan, sir?"

Your reporter attended Mayor Raúl Avila's presentation of $1500 to A. D. Gil Méndez and to Coach Emmy's softball champions at this year's honors banquet. A. D. Méndez thanked Mr. Jehú Malacara, president of the Klail City National Bank, for the new home-and-away uniforms.

This week's engagement announcements among Belken's graduating seniors are:

This reporter and Jay Jay Guzmán
Petronila Suárez and Tim Crowder
Debbie Rollins and Shane Taylor
Letti Hernández and Rogelio Chapa

Poly Sci major Alberto Munguía caused a minor uproar at the Chicano Cultural Committee—Mexican American Culture Center meeting at the Aztec/Maya Cultural Room. Munguía said that the officers want power and that attempts at seriousness were undermined by the officers' pompous attitudes. He apologized to the university's employees, who have to clean up the mess after every meeting.

Betsy 'Honey Bear' Magglo (Edgerton) shared Vale and Salu honors with Felipe Valverde (Jonesville). Congrats, guys.

What professor in Psych-Sosh is engaged to what professor in Music? Find out in Sept.

Belken senior Ivy Leaguers: Dora Almafuerte (Klail City/Brown), John Torres (Ruffing/Brown), Eduardo Elizondo (Flora/M.I.T.), Demetria Borchelt (Flads/Princeton), Betsy Maggio (Edgerton/Harvard), and Felipe Valverde (J'ville/Harvard).

Scholarships to UT and A&M in graduate work went to Al 'Sonny' Ríos (Klail City/UT), Cass Negrete (Klail

City/UT), and the Galván twins, Sandra and Claudia (J'ville/A&M)

A big hand for all. Those omitted should have contacted *The Bee* by May 10. Shame on you.

A SERIOUS MOMENT: Our prayers go to President Crowder.

Is there any senior who doesn't know Belken's alma mater? The words will be printed for you in the commencement brochure.

A thumping pat on the back to Eric Rodríguez and Tomasita Benítez for keeping their cool at the joint CCC/MACC meeting.

One final note. Abelardo Munguía apologized to everyone and asked me for a date. Told him I was engaged, and he hung up. That was cold. No, no, just kidding. Josie de la Viña is A. M.'s current squeeze.

This is my final column (my folks are delighted), and I'll go job hunting on Monday after graduation, depending, of course, on when I wake up.

See you at Perkins Pavilion's B.B.Q. Music by Rocky's Rockets.

The Chicano Cultural Club and the Mexican American Cultural Committee met at the Student Union and agreed to continue discussions on a merger of the two student organizations next fall.

An unidentified student laughed and said the talks would last longer than the Hundred Years War. Order was restored when the student apologized.

The Mexican American Cultural Committee reported that Texas Anglo fellow students Jodie Brazleton and Fritzie Ehrfurt, who were not present at the meeting, requested permission to become members of MACC. Parliamentarian Adelita Caballero stated there is nothing in the committee's bylaws forbidding any student, regardless of ethnicity, from becoming a member. She added that as a recognized student campus organization using university facilities for its meetings, MACC cannot deny membership.

The previously unidentified student, Alberto Munguía, said he welcomed them as long as they were cute, adding that being cute should not be an impediment. He then said both clubs needed to chill out and advised them to get their sh_t together. He left the meeting, giving everyone half of the victory sign.

Order was restored, and MACC's Glafira Osorio moved and Eric Rodríguez, a member of both organizations, seconded the Brazleton-Ehrfurt motion. It passed unanimously.

The organizations in this, their final semester meeting, congratulated Belken's Women's Softball Champions. The captains, Petra Anzaldúa, Joylene St. John, and Nelly Garza, attended as representatives of the championship team.

The CCC reported it had hand-delivered a message of condolence to Ms. Susan Crowder regarding the serious illness affecting President Nicholas T. Crowder. The CCC voted Professor Amada Ruelas (School of Social Work) as best Chicana professor. A certificate to that effect will be presented to Professor Ruelas next term. MACC voted Asst. Prof. Ismael Espinosa (Education) as best Mexican American instructor and Dr. Chickie Ríos (Education) as the outstanding Hispanic professor. Official MACC letters of recognition were mailed to Education Dean Pablo Esparza.

The CCC and the MACC invited all students to the Pachanga-mix at Perkins Pavilion following the commencement exercises on May 22.

Parents, spouses, family members, and guests are invited to celebrate and congratulate this year's graduating seniors.

For the first time in their history, MACC and the CCC combined this year's membership dues to help defray expenses for the Pachanga ($320).

# THE FACULTY
## III

# THE FACULTY

## I

Pancreatic cancer, I hear.
Prostate.
Oh.

•

Kit? Kit Brothers is his own worst enemy.
Not while I'm alive.
Really, Chris you should footnote someone else's wisecracks.

•

Bruce Kyle? He's only the Head of a department, for God's sakes.
I'm not informed as to the Almighty's actions, but Kyle *looks* like a president.

•

Okay, okay. But remember Wild Bill.
Yes, and who can forget that breath?

•

Our regents, all in all, are dedicated.
Yes, to the proposition that any donkey can be president.
Crowder a donkey?
Think a woman would do?
Agnes Gibson thinks so.
My lady looks so gentle and so pure.

That's nice.

That's Dante.

Look, if Agnes had her way, everyone would wear chastity belts.

That's harsh.

●

Well, does anyone know anything?

In a word, no. And, I don't care.

You should, you should care.

You and I will have this conversation again in five, six years.

●

It's the uncertainty of it all.

No. The sun will rise out of the east. Some students will be late, others absent, and all will provide exceptional excuses.

I really don't want to be like you, Dan.

Not to worry, and the name is Don.

●

What about the students? What do they want?

They want to graduate, get a job, and get the hell out of here.

Why, that. . . that's awful.

The poor are very different from you and me.

●

Do you know how the funding formula works?

What formula?

A three-hour course in Education is worth less than an English course, which is worth less than History; the sciences beat all.

And who came up with that little effort?

The University of Colorado.

Now there's a model to follow.

●

Oh, oh. There goes the V.P. for Administrative Services.

You're new. He's called Wild Bill.

As the Irishman said, "as fine a man as ever robbed the help-less."

What Irishman?

A character named Charles Carmody.

Never heard of him.

I'm shocked.

•

No, thanks, I'll have the tea.

I know that waiter. Who is he?

Grad student. One of Brothers' master's students working on *German Literature and Reunification of Germany, 1987-1989.* Who will then recommend him to the Big Ten—Wisconsin, I'll warrant.

He'll freeze up there, Ben.

He'll blossom like a tulip in winter.

•

It doesn't matter. I bet French'll get screwed again.

Spanish is the first and second language here.

I have no idea what induced me to Belken.

A job offer, Albert.

Up yours.

That's what I like, scholarly repartee.

•

Shoot, it's like living in the Dark Ages.

Which weren't so dark. Dante, Petrarach, Boccaccio.

And don't forget John of Salisbury and Giraldus Cambrensis.

Oh, let's stop talking like professors.

But that's what we are, Childs. Professors.

Look, I've been here twenty-one years, the same as you, and we've gone through seven presidents.

Eight. You're forgetting Colvin.

Colvin's one semester must be a world's record.

Oh, Colvin, we hardly knew ye.

•

I have two students who've read and understood—under-grads, mind you—*Absalom* and *Sound and Fury*.

The rest?

West of Mars, sad to say; these two and I sat and talked in my office for an hour and a half. They made sense. You know, there is such a thing as cultural geography. They kept making references to the Valley, to the Mexican Revolution of 1910, and relating the history of the South, Mississippi, and the Valley's closed society. Amazing.

I'm glad, Cliff.

I was elated. Went home and Sandy and I dined at the Camelot.

Way to go, Cliff Benson.

You realize you're living beyond your wife's means, don't you?

Ahhh, those two kids were like an electrical charge, you know that?

One's a poet, Cliff. He writes for Toby Rubinsky, and Toby is high on him.

Now, that's praise.

Few and far between, but that oyster pops and you find not one but two pearls; whomever is selected as president will be as nothing compared to this.

English majors?

No, they're both in Economics.

# THE FACULTY

## II

Physics got one new line and Chemistry two.

How about Anthro and Sosh?

One each for this year and one each for next year.

●

The people in Biology? No, no lines. It's a matter of critical
mass.

No students, no professorial lines.

The way it should be.

The way it wasn't.

Now you're talking.

●

Crowder's been here seven, eight years. Anybody notice any
changes?

Try this: I'm teaching six hours less, and I have more time for
my lab assistants.

But you also got a three-year $300,000 grant, Uxley.

That's right, and Javier Delgado brought in a quarter of a million. You can't expect those guys in Liberal Arts to raise that kind
of money.

But they've got Christopher Brother. . .

Brothers. . .

Right, and he goes after his Lib Arts alums. I bet that's hard
work.

He's gotten good results, though.

Think he'd make a good president?

I do.

So do I. But, does he want the job?

Clarence Wright would nominate him.

Amen to that, Charlie, but I wouldn't do it without his permission.

●

The Sussmans donated two baby grands. The Lord knows we've needed them.

Whose Lord?

Oh, God. Yours, mine, and theirs. . . Go on, Manny.

It's frustrating. I've just lost two more talented students. Again. One to North Texas and the other to Florida: a violinist and a pianist.

That's tough, Manny.

Hell, I'm not quitting. Mel is trying his best for us, and he's no quitter.

●

So you're leaving us, Larry?

At the end of the term. It's been a good five years here, and I'll miss you guys.

The best of luck to you. I just heard it this morning.

UC Irvine's bound to have some Texas students who'd want to come back.

Yeah, build up our master's program.

That's a promise I'll keep.

●

Well, it's a good thing I'm retiring. Things're just getting too hectic here. I'm sixty-seven, boys, and that's it. See you, I'm off to class.

Who's that?

Colby Triplett. . . One of the old guys. Hates Mexicans and has been here for twenty-odd years.

One of the old hires, Frank. Belken was recruiting left and right, then.

Mostly right.

That's a terrible pun.

I'm not sorry he's retiring. You ought to hear the students.

It's common knowledge, Ramón. Tells stories, jokes, and every kid gets an A. Great teacher reports from them but not from the serious kids. Yes, tenure is a wonderful thing.

It is, and I'm for it. Triplett's not alone, but age catches up with the good and the bad.

As I said, I, for one, won't miss him.

You're not alone.

Ha, I wouldn't be chairman in that department for one million dollars.

●

Another day, another dullard, there goes Wild Bill.

Yeah, he's a nice old guy.

Wild Bill loves disciples.

Unh. Not my idea of a Messiah. Pass the salt, will you?

●

Congratulations.

Add mine to those.

Thanks, I appreciate it.

You earned it, no question.

Thanks again. I've a fishing buddy who has a book and a contract for a second book, and got passed over. Didn't even make it out of the department.

History?

English.

Hey.

•

Congrats on the softball championship, Emmy.

Yeah, Emilia Uresti, voted Coach of the Year in the conference.

Good for Belken.

Love those new uniforms, Em.

Me, too. Snazzy.

Snazzy? My mom uses that word.

Well, I'm old enough to be your mom.

That's telling her, Gerda.

The uniforms were the President's work and the Klail National Bank.

Yeah, but home and away uniforms, with no state funding.

Not for sports, not in this state, anyway.

That little runt.

Petra Anzaldúa? Best lefty I've had here. Her folks are tops, too. And there's a senior Anzaldúa at Klail High coming up.

Think UT'll grab her?

Sure, if they could find the Valley.

And that sweet double-play combination, wow.

Yeah, that's Pris and Estela Blanco. They're from across, you know.

Barrones?

No, little Control; there's a pretty good alum base there.

•

Lucy Martínez is directing the senior play, you all.

I've recommended that De León girl as Regan.

Which De León is that?

She was one of the old ladies in *Arsenic and Old Lace* last year.

*Lear's* a tough play.

I bet Lucy knows every line.

And who was in this year's one-acter?

Terry Wade and that Donaldson boy.

Ha! There are three Donaldsons and they're all weird.

Smart though, right? This one's J.D.

Bright? Oh yes, and they work hard. Single mom?

Yeah. Her name is Mary Helen Boyd.

Divorced.

Oh no. Catholics, big time. Her husband was a train engineer. You remember that wreck two, three years back?

Oh, God, yes. What a mess. All three kids serve as altar boys.

The pastor is Juan José de la Cruz. His family owns a laundry chain in the Valley.

You Catholic, Lolly?

Since I was hours old.

So you know the family?

Oh, yeah. Father J. J. and my older brother Roy were the best of friends at St. Joe's.

We have any number of St. Joe kids here, don't we?

That's Marist training for you.

It's not Jesuit?

No, no. The Marist Brothers came here in 1853. My cousin Rafe says Brother Allemand is 146 years old.

Oh, God.

Oh no, he's a bit older.

Please.

●

Here comes your boss, Emmy.

Hi, Gil.

Trophies came in. They spelled your name right.

What?

Trophies came in. They spelled your name right.

What?

It's a standing joke, Marie.

Is next Monday okay for you? The Kiwanis Club would like

to host this year's banquet. Your seniors graduate next Sunday,
and I think they'd appreciate the send off.
That's very thoughtful of them, Gil. Thanks.
Bye, you all.
Bye, Coach.

●

Can I join in?
Sure thing, Jack. Here, let me get my things out of the way.
See you, guys.
Any news?
Talking about Bruce Kyle. He's getting married.
Boy, he didn't lose any time, did he?
Seven years, you kidding? That first union was bound to dissolve.
Who's the bride to be?
Her name is Beatriz Guerra, niece to a regent.
Way to go, Bruce.
That first wife was a case.
Social climber, was she?
Steeplechaser. As for Beatriz Guerra, she's a stunner.
Sharp, too. C.P. A. Owns her own firm, the whole package.
I ought to get out more often.

●

Any news on Nick?
A slow death, Mac.
Jesus.

●

My baccalaureate? Physics and math at old Texas A&I.
Me too. Wonder why we didn't run across each other?
You were a senior when I came in.
Who'd you work with, Wes Paul or Georgie Schultz?
Paul, the first two years, and the last two with the old man.
What'd you think?

Best undergraduate preparation I could've gotten.

Yeah, we got our money's worth, all right.

You know, late in the fall, before I finished, he said M.A. at U.T., but the Ph.D. at a third school. Do it, Moreno.

Yeah, he always told seniors that. I do too for our master's.

So do I. Hey, ah, he make any mention about AP courses in Math?

Oh, yeah. Called us apes.

Funny old guy. I tell my students the same: two more degrees? Two different schools.

Oh, here comes Twenhafel. Irv, over here.

Well! I thought Vangie Peña was going to split a gut.

Look, Guy Hoppe has no business. . .

As they say, he minds everybody's but his own.

•

Who'll be your next chair over there?

God, I hope it's either Jim Ward or Phil Godfrey, either one.

Hugo Sánchez straightened out our department in one year. He sure as hell did.

Trouble?

Troubles. Drugs, drinking, porno films, students—choose the order you want.

Heard about the students.

That's disgusting, it's unpleasant, and you can add distressing to that.

Chandler wouldn't have done it that way.

No. Glenn is a nice guy, but you needed a hard nose like Hugo to clean those stables.

The parents?

The students were over twenty-one.

Still, it's a mess.

A big job for Public Affairs.

Yeah, it was a mess. We nearly went into receivership. That would have set Biology back four graduating classes. It was that serious.

Well? Didn't you guys say anything?

We talked to them. Told them, repeatedly. Bill called them in.

Forget it, some people won't listen.

They were asking for it.

Our chair called the Dean and resigned, and the Dean recommended Hugo Sánchez as Interim Chair. Hugo was directing three master's theses and someone took his two classes, and he went to work.

He sure did. Deposed I don't know how many people with Belken lawyers present. Before the end of the coming fall term, he was ready, and out came the broom.

Vacuum cleaner was more like it.

Man, those guys from Chemistry don't fool around.

He then called those jackasses to his office and. . .

Yeah, I heard. . . Real pros, those two. "And who is going to teach our courses in the fall?"

That, said Hugo, is something that shouldn't worry either one of you.

Papers didn't say anything.

You're right. Nick Crowder took care of that.

Pressure?

No, the truth, and the editor said it wasn't worth printing.

And the two guys?

Crowder said that was up to them. If they wanted the full story in the open, they'd get it.

Damn. That must've been hell for their families.

It always is, but some people don't think.

It's hell, though.

●

Heard Kit Brothers went to bat for an assistant prof.

He interfered with a departmental no-tenure recommendation?

No. Better than that. Got him a job elsewhere.

Was it that colleague from English?

He's the one. Is that creamer empty?

And how did you learn about the job, Craven?

If I told you, my source of information would dry up.

Rubbish, the staff knows everything.

I'm not saying anything, but his name is Elliott Chalmers.

Is he related to Percy?

No idea.

Good for Kit, say I.

I'll second that.

●

The Klail National is offering good rates on car loans.

Why not, they've got eight or nine Belken State accounts.

They've also got the best-looking tellers in town.

And *that* is a non-denial denial.

●

Who's eating with the Deans over there?

That's Sam Atteberry, his law firm represents the System.

Most probably about the unpleasantness at Biology.

I bet it is—I see Hugo's with them.

That clinches it. Unpleasant? Stupid, John.

There's Percy Chalmers. Move over, Ed, make room.

Gentlemen.

Sit down, sit down. What's new?

Grace and I are throwing a little barbecue for our softball champs.

You a fan?

I bet Perse hasn't missed three games since he got here ten years ago.

Oh, I've missed a few. We decided a Saturday afternoon since commencement's on a Sunday this year.

Who's your caterer?

Lee Castañeda. . . and H. & H. furnished the meat.

Free, *gratis*?

They're big supporters of Belken.

Gotta go, guys. See you, Perse.

Sounds nice. Too bad Nick's not going to be there.

Ah, Coach Emmy will most likely lead us in prayer during grace, don't you think?

She's a winner.

●

Anybody not hear about Emmy's team?

I'll say, a championship for Belken.

She's a builder, and that won't be the last blue ribbon and trophy.

Hey, there's Andy Tullis looking for a table.

Tullis. Andy, over here.

# THE FACULTY

## III

You guys need to back me up. What's wrong with you? We've got to stick together.

God helps those who help themselves.

Now what the hell is that supposed to mean?

It means this: your Ph.D. is six years old, and you haven't published a book.

Yes, I have. I sent you all a copy.

It's a vanity press publication, Beto.

It's still a book.

But you paid to have it published.

Not only that, of the two articles and the monograph on your vita, none is from a refereed journal.

What a bunch of friends you are.

If you'd stop politicking. . .

It's important to the community.

The community. . . the community expects us to work, just like they do.

He's right, Beto. This isn't the sixties or the seventies, man. We have more kids in school, some are sharper than we were at that age.

Bull crap.

Bull reality.

David won the Belton Prize in History and it's a TCU Press publication, and Ricardo's book from Texas Tech Press is in its fifth printing.

Sixth.

You see? We went to bat for you after your third-year review.

Yeah. We stuck our necks, put our names on the line, we gave assurances.

Yeah, see here, Beto, you. . .

Ha! What a bunch of friends you turned out to be.

You're blaming the wrong people.

What do you mean?

Look in the mirror. Let's go, guys.

●

EXCERPTS from the Faculty Council and the Faculty Senate in an Extraordinary Joint Session.

*Professor Victor Polacz*: Madam Chairman, the Mathematics Department hired Assistant Professor Mauricio Vásquez, who did not disappoint; he rose to Associate Professor in three years. Appointed chair of departmental recruitment, Professor Vásquez brought in Assistant Professors Ralph Daikus, a recent Cal graduate, and Lionel de la Torre from Northwestern.

For the record: We're a small school in a small system, but we can grow our own. We hire assistant professors, and it's sink or swim for them, the way it should be.

I will now address Professors Homer Tulke and Ramiro Moya from Chemistry, and Physics, respectively, regarding minority hires. It's a simple question, and it's not only time, it's past time. Thank you, Madam Chairman.

[Brief summaries of Professors Tulke's and Moya's report.]

TULKE: Chemistry was assigned two lines by Dean Bromley, and we invited five candidates, two of which were minority recruitments under the target of opportunity provisions as authorized by the Board of Regents. Of the three majority population visitors, Chemistry hired one nonminority and one minority as assistant professors.

*Professor Polacz*: Thank you, Professor Tulke.

MOYA: Physics was also awarded two lines one year ago, but we tendered no offers of employment. A request to keep the lines for this year was granted by Dean Bromley. Last fall, ads were placed in three national professional journals; the department's Executive Committee invited six; two minorities were selected. One declined and one accepted. The majority hire selected was Assistant Professor Jeffrey Boykin who accepted the position, as did Assistant Professor Arturo Leal.

*Professor Polacz*: Thank you, Professor Moya. Madam Chairman, I have a further progress report.

As concerns the English department's continuing policy of aggressive searches for minority candidates, the English chair, Professor Darley, requested I enter the following as part of the record: Assistant Professor Amelia de Hoyos, a specialist in Medieval Studies, was hired last December to succeed retiring Professor David Thomas. Assistant Professor Effie García, a Romanticist, was hired last December to succeed retiring professor Louisa Mae Schons. The Department of Modern Languages reported that its Spanish section, once again, has failed to fill the two assistant professor slots availed to it by Dean Christopher Brothers. The Council's ad hoc committee on the College of Liberal Arts' efforts on minority hires reports that this is the third year those slots have not been filled by the Spanish section.

One consequence of this failure is the burden placed on teaching assistants at the master's level to assume extra classes of first- and second-year Spanish. A corollary consequence is that the master's students have delayed completion of their theses or programs by one semester and some by a full school year. This is regrettable, and the ad hoc committee expresses deep disappointment.

After my report to Dean Brothers, he, orally and in writing, assured me that he would meet with the Department Chair of Modern Languages before the end of the Spring semester, that is, three weeks hence, when I present my report on what the Dean considers his serious concerns, given, among other matters, that Belken State University is a traditional minority institution.

Madam Chairman, this concludes my two-year appointment by the Faculty Council on matters concerning fair-hire practices for most talented candidates for our institution under regental provisions.

*Madam Chairman Jeffords*: The Chair recognizes the yeoman work and effort of Political Science Professor Victor Polacz. Thank you.

I have a letter from Professor Andy Tullis of the Faculty Council; the Council voted unanimously that Professor Irving Twenhafel represent the Council as a member of the Presidential Search Committee. The second letter comes from the Faculty Senate and reads as follows: By acclamation, the Faculty Senate selected Professor Hugo Sánchez of the Chemistry department as its representative as a member of the Presidential Search Committee.

I will now entertain a motion that a letter be sent to Vice President Robert Rhodes of this joint meeting.

The motion was passed unanimously.

Robert Huddleston, Ph.D.
Mathematics Department
Recording Secretary and
Parliamentarian

# THE FACULTY

## IV

Professor Avila to see you, sir.

Thank you, have him come in, please.

Afternoon. Want the door closed?

Would you please?

Well, how are things in Secondary Ed?

Not good, sorry to say.

Oh?

Yes, sir. She turned us down.

Not enough money, was that it?

No, she didn't mention money. She was awarded tenure last week.

Last week? We tendered the offer in plenty of time.

I don't know what to say. I didn't talk to her.

How'd you find out?

Dina Fernández received an e-mail—not a phone call, nor a letter. An e-mail, and Dina forwarded it to me.

I see. Hmph. She was playing the game and used our offer as leverage.

I see. If Belken wants her, then why don't we?

Something like that. You think she used us, don't you, Mando?

I don't know. What do you think?

I think she was playing the game, that's all.

Well, I don't like those types of games.

I don't either, but there you are.

Just thought I'd come by and say thanks. I guess I'm disappointed because she didn't talk to me. I mean, I've been behind her all the way. But I also want to thank you for going to bat for us again.

•

You guys hear about Charlie at the Faculty Senate? Wants us and
the Council to approach the Regents about naming a hall for
President Crowder.

That's not a bad idea.

I think he's grandstanding.

He's not. Charlie Figueroa's no hypocrite. Since Nick Crowder's
been here, we've gone from three *raza* profs to thirty-three in
Liberal Arts, the sciences, and Math. That's four a year, and
with more on the way.

Aw, hell, you've always stood up to him.

Who's him? Charlie or the President?

Both. Bryan Clack says . . .

Bryan Clack is a frustrated, troublemaking, time-server. He's
been an associate prof for seventeen years, and he'll retire as
one.

Talk about a drone.

You don't know him as I do. You really don't.

Clack's Claque. There's a bunch like that on every campus.

I'll tell him you said that.

Do, Ruben. And while you're at it, turn on your computer to
Belken's Web page and look up his vita. Some fifteen projects
in progress, and half are twelve years old, and none published.

What are you, the campus cop?

And take this with you, tell him I said he's an unproductive
parasite.

Jesus Christ, David. I can't.

No, you can't. Was it your idea or Clack's?

What are you talking about?

Criticism of Charlie Figueroa's proposal, that's what.

He said Chicanos should stick together.

So we're his new project, are we?

Look, you're the oldest one of us here, and we, I mean, I, I
thought . . .

Excuse me, I have a class in about ten minutes.

Wait a minute, please.

Chuy, it's a simple problem of arithmetic: you have an academic future, and Clack doesn't. Now, you must excuse me.

What about the rest of you?

We're leaving.

●

Congratulations, Ernie. That's quite an accomplishment, and thanks for calling.

My pleasure, sir.

(Renate Vaudrey's voice comes over the intercom.)

Dr. Espinosa to see you, sir.

Have him come in.

Good afternoon, Dean.

It's good to see you.

Thank you. I've a vita here from an assistant prof. Her name is Linda Magallanes, and she's asking me about our line in Curriculum and Instruction.

It's an application.

No, I don't think so, sir.

The law says it is. We have a position, it's been advertised, and she wrote to you.

Good Lord. Anyway, here's the vita.

Mmmmm. She's been at three institutions in five years. I don't see any publications, Ismael. Can you account for that?

No, I can't.

She sure goes to a lot of conferences, though.

That's where I met her, at the South Central Ed Conference last fall.

Has she written to Chickie Ríos?

She didn't say, sir. She e-mailed me saying she heard we have an opening in C&I, and sent the vita.

It doesn't look good to move around this much in such a short time. What can you tell me about her? Excuse me. . .

Sir?

No publications and her Ed.D. is four years old. Angela de la Rosa
and Chickie just brought in half a million dollars for the
improvement of secondary education in Texas and for the rest
of the nation. And you just saw Adolfo Gavito's garnering his
five-year grant from the Texas Agency; this is important to the
Southern System. And you had two big grants yourself, aside
from an important book last year on elementary education.

Thank you.

I don't see anything here. Looks like a trial balloon, but you
should treat this as an application. We don't want it coming
back to bite C&I in the future.

I see.

One more thing, nothing in this vita shows her as a promising candidate.

What do you suggest?

Acknowledge receipt of the vita by e-mail, and if she calls or
writes, e-mail her that you've sent her vita to the college's
Search Committee. Walk this over to C&I and give it to
Chickie's secretary. And be careful, Ismael.

Sir?

We're not a placement agency.

Thank you.

How's your work?

We've interviewed 150 low, middle, and upper-income Mexican
American families from ten cities and towns in the Valley.

Sounds promising.

I've got a good team. Took us over a month to agree on the fifty
questions that'll be used to establish attitudes past and present toward education of the target group.

That's what I mean.

Sir?

You've devised a strong, systematic questionnaire that, after your
analysis, will provide important information on ten million

Hispanic families in the Southwest regarding education.
Thank you, sir.
That's solid, sound, coherent material you'll be providing for the
taxpayer.
We've a way to go since it's a longitudinal study.
The way it should be. Anything else?
No, but thank you, and . . .
Yes?
Thank you for the advice. I appreciate it.
Take the vita to C&I and have them file it.
I really don't know her that well. I mean, I met her at a confer-
ence.
Ismael, you're not a water carrier. Do keep your Chairman
informed regarding your study. If the local paper gets wind of
it, he can refer the reporter to you. Keep up the good work.
Thank you, sir.

●

Sam Atteberry and his lawyers just left.
Yep. That leaves only Hugo and Bill Bromley at their table.
Does Hugo ever smile, guys?
Hey, that's funny, what do you mean?
He's smiling now.
I guess it means the Biology affair's been resolved.

# THE FACULTY

## V

I heard Brothers fired the one in charge of the Spanish section.
Just like that? Fired, fired?
Well, he told the language chair to remove the guy in charge of
the Spanish section.
Whatever for?
Read the Council and Senate minutes, Petersen.
Look, Pete, those guys have sat on two lines for three years.
That's criminal.
I'll say. . .
You know,  I was talking to Raab, the one who teaches German
and French, he says Brothers gave French one of those lines.
Kit also added a three-hour teaching load to two full profs.
Well, he's in trouble now.
Wrong end of the stick, Pete. It's the Chair who's on notice. As
for those two, whomever they are, they'll go back to teaching
three and four, maybe even four classes per term.
Don't they have T.A.s?
Sure, and they've been overloaded and overworked for some time
now.
Brothers has every right to lean on those guys. You don't produce,
you get what's coming to you.
What you're saying is that it's unfair treatment of the T.A.s.
Unfair? It's exploitation in the worst way. It's delayed some mas-
ter's students' graduation from one to two semesters.
Where'd you get this from?
It's common knowledge.

Well, Bryan Clack says. . .
Please, we're eating.

●

Hey, I was just talking to Shirley Bell.
Is she the one in Psych?
No, that's Sherry Bell, no relation.
What'd she say?
Brothers is going to revamp Modern Languages.
Revamp?
That's a serious step.
In what way, did she say?
Well, she didn't specify.
Wisner, you call that news?

●

Boy, things are going to pop in Modern Languages. You all hear
that Brothers spent three hours with the Chair?
No, we've been talking about the President.
Oh, still bad?
He's dying, Benson.
Any word from Bruce Kyle about the Regents?
Dream on, brother.
Bryan Clack says. . .
What now?
Well, he says the new President's going to be a Mexican American.
Where'd you hear that?
I'm telling you, Clack. . .
Where'd he hear that?
Bryan says he heard it from Bruce Kyle.
Yeah, and last week I shot three holes in one. Get off it, Riley.
But. . .
No buts, please.

•

How did Dean Borchers get two lines over in Business?

Ready? He's the Ambrose Clarke Chair as well as the Minerva Hale Chair, right? Well, gave up one of 'em to get the candidate.

Can he do that?

I'm sure he checked with Rhodes.

Why Rhodes?

In case you haven't heard, he's still the VP for Academic Affairs.

What I meant was, can he do that?

And Bob Rhodes checked with the President.

Boy, that must be some candidate.

Try this, fifteen years with one of New York's top ad agencies.

And don't forget the money.

Big bucks, eh?

Look, Business has money, gets money, and goes after more.

They've also been accredited since Ned Borchers came here fifteen years ago.

Wow.

•

English put up a map of the U.S. marked with pins and names of their Masters who've been accepted for the doctorate. Pretty impressive.

That'd give me incentive if I were a major.

Ted Darley settled that department down in two semesters flat.

Were they in danger of going into receivership?

No, not that serious.

That's right. They were rambunctious and argumentative and *The Belken Bee* was getting its info from the inside.

And then, Kit Brothers dropped Huntley after his first term, and English elected Darley.

Big to-do, eh?

Nope. As smooth a transition as you've ever seen.

Listen, Kit Brothers doesn't interfere unless a department is really screwed up. They just needed a change.

Take Darley long?

As I said, two semesters, and that was it.

•

You want news? The Klail City National awarded three five-thousand-dollar scholarships to Lib Arts.

That president? He's got a funny name, Noddy.

That's the big cheese. The president is Jehú Malacara.

That name's not common either.

Old Testament. Named one scholarship for his wife and one each for their two kids.

An old Belken alum?

No, I don't think so.

Really, Treviño, if you're not going to read the Klail City paper, you should at least read *The Bee*.

That scholarship's just the beginning, you all. That banker serves on a committee made up of Mexican American businessmen, lawyers, doctors, accountants, and so on.

That's nice, real nice.

Whomever succeeds Nick Crowder better not drop the damn ball with the influential Mexican American community. Our kids need all the help they can get.

Amen. They probably work more than they study.

It's not right, but that's the truth of it.

•

Boy, I remember when Education was a laugh. Everybody got A's.

Too many still do, and it's those Education courses. They should take more classes in the Liberal Arts.

In English, French, and so on?

Right.

Ha! What they should concentrate on in those departments is how to read and write. Some thinking would help.

That's been going around since I started some twenty-five years ago.

That new Dean is a hard nose, I hear.

You got some proof on that?

I'll tell you, he didn't exactly throw the guy out of his office, but . . .

Was it a Mexican American prof?

Right. He told him to straighten up, to publish refereed articles, to stop politicking, and to stop using his class as a forum.

And to stop listening to Bryan Clack.

Poor Clack, again.

I'm afraid Bryan brings that on himself.

Manny's right. Was it an assistant prof, by the way?

From what I hear.

That kid should listen to the Dean.

The Dean got that Mexican American woman who came from Barnard.

On the nose.

She came in as chairperson, and she's a Valley girl.

Not bad for a Belken baccalaureate. Checked her vita, too.

And?

Came out clean.

Good for her.

# THE REGENTS
## IV

Regent Eulalio "Lalo" Guerra cradled the phone softly and stared at it with a look of heartfelt disgust. Calls are important when you want them, bothersome when you don't; the last call was one of the bothersome ones: not his business, university business.

It's started, he sighed. We need a Mexican American president, Lalo, you know that. Of course he knew it, and, looking at the phone, better than you. He rose from his armchair, walked to the outer office, and ordered coffee; oh, and no more calls. The name and number will do, thank you. A Mexican American. Sure, but there were few Leo Flores' on the market. The office seekers, to quote Dean Brothers, have always been in long supply. He'd rely on that dean of Liberal Arts for advice. He then thought on Nick Crowder. A good man; hell, a fine man. The search had started with no Mexican American applicants, but that, he remembered, changed soon enough.

That dean would be a good man, a solid candidate. But would he want the job? Funny people, academics. If someone wants the job too much, he can't be that good. If no interest shown, that would be among the ones to seek, interview, invite to campus for a visit, meet the wife, the family, show them around the town, and then get down to the real business at ten a.m. promptly the following day.

Ha! Tom Landry once said, when asked about kickers, "You can always get a kicker." True, what he wanted was quarterbacks, something you can't always get. Was that dean a kicker or was he quarterback material? No point asking my niece Beatrice. A good head on those swimmer's shoulders, but prejudiced in favor. And yet, and yet, social friendship aside, her assessment would be worth something. Someone to keep in mind.

As for that phone call. . . Nothing to be gained from that quarter; a Mexican American, Lalo, a Mexican American. Sure, like that VP in Engineering and the one in Business that were let go. Hopeless, the two of them. My Anglo friends wanted them—and to heck with ability. Well, no more, not while I'm a regent, and that's assured for another four-year term, at least.

Yeah, me, Lalo Guerra, Mr. Big Shot. Who am I kidding? I'm plain old Lalo. Lucky Lalo, they call me. Start off as a clerk with Boetticher's Grocery, move on to Glover's, and old man Horace Glover makes me store manager. Now there was a first. Gladys Glover dies of uterine cancer, Horace decides to quit and leaves me the store, and I own it at age thirty. Lucky Lalo, that's me. But Horace Glover knew what he wanted: his name on the sign and me as owner. Horace Junior was killed in a motor accident. I saw him die and held his hand to the last at Mercy. I remember the young Lalo who cried.

Built the store up, hired more people, my own accountant, and Klail had its first and only Super Market. On the side, the mom-and-pop store which, like Topsy, just grew: one, two, three, four, a dozen, up and down the Valley.

Nothing to it. The accountant said, sell the stores, buy land; the Valley's bound to grow. And I did, and the Valley grew. Did well, too. My attorney said, give money to the politicians. Which side? The two in the runoffs; good old Texas and its one-party state in those days. Much like it is now with the Reps in power. Nothing lasts, however. Public anger will take care of them.

What's that to me? Nothing. It's Belken State that's important. Close to a ninety-two percent Mexican American enrollment. It needs the best, not friends of the Regents and not this Regent. Wonder what my friend Traudi Moeckle will do? West Texas cowgirl, tougher than one-dollar steak. Too bad about that nephew of hers. Tough.

Leo Flores should be calling with his recommendation. That's someone worth listening to. Leo: "Mr. Guerra, in the last six years, we've hired two Mexican American mathematicians, two physicists, a chemist, and a dean for the Music School, and we've lost all six. We can't compete with the UC system, why, even when they're broke. California's got the money, the power, the libraries, and they can hire graduate students for their new hires to work on their labs or whatever they want.

"And now the Big Ten's in the hunt for Mexican Americans. And then we lost the one chemist to Brown, and that brought in the Ivy League. We'll keep it at, though. I wasn't hired to come here to retire, to hire three maids from across the river, to week-end at Padre Island, and so on.

"We'll get some good people again, Regent."

But California offered him a chancellorship, and that was that. We lucked out on Crowder. I never did ask Leo how he and Crowder met. Probably at the Rockefeller Foundation or at the Carnegie or something. Wonder if Crowder's condition has gotten out? Sure, all it takes is a phone call from a nurse to her mother, best friend, whatever.

But he's not dead yet, and he's showed up for work every day. We were looking and planning, and he gave sound advice in the search.

Traudi Moeckle stepped up to the sidewalk facing the Belken County Courthouse thinking of her conversation with the Chief Inspector. "All business, that policeman," she said to herself as she hailed a taxi.

Part of the job, I imagine. And the questioning cum interview cum conversation began with a question: Was Gary involved in drugs, as far as you've been able to find out? Well, he sized me up on that one, and yes, we knew Gary was gay and from time to time, a transvestite too. And then he waited. I said nothing and he went on: Mrs. Moeckle (and that neutral voice, much like a kind country doctor)—am I pronouncing that right?—thank you. Mrs. Moeckle, it was made to look like an argument between gays that led to a homicide. You see, and he looked me in the eye, the scene pointed to that. Dr. Paredes counted sixty-seven stab wounds. A small knife. And, of course, I had to ask: Did he count each one? She, he said, and yes, she did. After doing so, she had her assistant take a count as well. They agreed. He saw I wasn't giving any ground, and he then offered me a cup of coffee or tea. Just like that, the way my Ralph had of changing but not really changing the subject, smooth like. Staying on point, but letting the facts sink in. He chose a mug on the rack and I said, straight, no cream, no sugar. He nodded almost absently and turned. It's high grade, we've no decaf in this office. I smiled, I couldn't help it. He wasn't being standoffish, let alone insensitive, it was the way he moved, not giving himself or anything away. He was a nephew, I understand? Yes, I'm a widow woman. And here I was reverting to country talk. You may smoke, if you wish. He opened a drawer and slid a spotless ashtray over. And he waited.

You're a regent at Belken State, aren't you? I replied I was

and added that Belken along with Jarvis and Bonham State
formed our system. Avoided the clutches of UT and A&M, did
you? I smiled and said yes, as I nodded. Was this some sub-
terfuge? Was this a way of disarming me? I then asked where he
went to school. He said UT and, when pressed, UT Law. Passed
bar? Oh, yes. Became a cop, though. I finished my coffee and
waited. I didn't know where, but I guess, perhaps knew, we were
going somewhere. Your nephew was strangled and then stabbed.
He died when he struck his head on the wall heater. I'm calling
the evidence room. As the nearest relative in this district, his
effects belong to you; we need you to identify them. He stopped
suddenly and asked, in that pleasant but efficient voice, you don't
have to look at them; however, it'd be a help to the D.A.'s office.
What came next was another tremor. For the newspapers, this is
an open-and-shut case. Your nephew may have been gay, I never
met him, but we suspect the homicide was staged to look like a
homosexual rage murder. The number of stabbings, the mess in
the living room, but the murderer overdid it: he made a mess of
the kitchen, but the bedroom was untouched. Murderers are usually amateurs, Mrs. Moeckle. The crime scene is part of the evidence. You see, it points to something. We have the murderer, and
he was remanded to custody without bail. He's not a known
homosexual; three detectives showed his photograph to men and
women at gay bars in the area and no one knew him. I guess you
know your nephew was fond of using his initials, F.G.L., on his
personal property, watch, ring, and so on. . . I nodded and said that
the L stood for his father, Longley. Well, there's a piece of a cheap
I.D. bracelet, and the man in custody says it isn't his. That's not
important, his are the only fingerprints on the bracelet, and the
D.A. will use that. The bracelet may have broken off during the
struggle. His defense will be self-defense, defending himself
against an aggressive homosexual. He stopped and raised his
hand. I know the law firm. The accused is the victim and so on.
Now, we've got him dead to rights. He's prone to violence, a num-

ber of arrests attest to that—the defense will object to this as prej-
udicial. They'll request a meeting with the judge and the prosecu-
tors in the judge's chambers. It's a ploy, Mrs. Moeckle; it's for the
jury. As a regent, your name will be in the papers. A photo, I
should imagine. You must say we met for I.D. purposes, which is
true. The university is looking or will begin a search for a new
president. That also means you'll be coming to town on a more
regular basis. Am I correct? Yes. The scenes he described were
emerging as if a series of photos. There will be a subpoena issued
by the defense and you'll be treated as a hostile witness and they
will harp on the gay issue. That's not debatable, but they are the
defense, and they will try anything. They'll come after you. Oh,
dear Lord, I then said a foolish thing: "Let them try." I regretted it
as soon as I popped off. They will. But there's something else:
they don't know you, as I think I do, and I don't care how many
witnesses they depose. You, in that witness stand, will not break,
will you? I ask because the questions will be offensively repeti-
tious, they will sneer for the jury's benefit: here's a witness, she's
sworn to tell the truth, etcetera, but how reliable and trustworthy
is she?

●

There was nothing else to say. I was being dismissed but without that freezing atmosphere that ends an unpleasant conversation. I walked toward the door and somehow he was there ahead
of me. I won't fold, I said, firmly. Mrs. Moeckle, he said, and just
as firmly, I knew that beforehand. Oh? I'm a friend of Joe
Eubanks. Completely disarmed, all I could say was: You lawyers
do stick together, don't you?

"Goodbye, Chief Inspector."

"Mrs. Moeckle."

●

Joseph Orr Edwards Eubanks was reviewing recent actuarial tables and away from his desk when his administrative secretary's voice came over the phone.

"Sir? Sir?"

"Yes, Lillian, what is it?"

"Mr. Buenrostro's on line two."

"Milo? Aaron?"

"No, sir, the Chief Inspector."

"Thanks, Lillian, I'll take it in the library."

"Thank you, sir."

"Joe? Rafe. You're right, Mrs. Moeckle will do."

"Told you."

"A shame, but I did warn her about the dirty work when she's called to testify."

"She won't crack. What are you up to, anyway?"

"Going home. Thought I'd ring you up and give my thanks."

"Anytime."

"Anything, I can do…?"

A chuckle. "Oh, you will, Rafe. See you."

"Bye."

Traudi Moeckle, an heiress who married money, lost her husband, Ralph, after sixteen years of a happy, successful marriage. A do-gooder, friends and enemies alike called her, and they were right. Traudi worked on the side of the angels. Money to the local hospital (No, we don't want a wing or anything else named for us), money for the improvement of the local high school facilities (Yes, you understood correctly, no plaques, please), and her time, a commodity as valuable as her talents. And now, in her fourth and final year as a regent for the Southern State Universities System. It had been a sad three weeks with the loss of her favorite nephew—murdered—and now, the sad news of Nick Crowder's cancer. He offered to resign in January but stayed to help in the search for his replacement. He—God willing—would stay as emeritus to help his successor, provided his health. . .

What genes she inherited from her parents, a Buchbinder for a mother married to a Pittmann, were as strong as her sense of duty. And, it was this sense which drove her to call Joe Eubanks, her closest friend among the Regents. During the Regents' meetings, she'd call his private number.

•

"Traudi! Yes, please, do come on over. As soon as you get here, we'll have a salad at The Camelot. Oh. . ."

"Yes, I know, don't bother to knock."

This was reliable Joe Eubanks, friend, counsel, and soul mate who, with his money and that of Mexican businessmen from Barrones, across the river from Klail, established the Ralph Moeckle Belken State University International Museum.

Her brief visit with the Chief Inspector had comforted her, it had also left her without being able to read Buenrostro's charac-

ter, something she had been able to do—not a common talent—
since childhood in Colorado City. But she trusted the Chief
Inspector since Joe had recommended him, and that, for Traudi
Moeckle, was what counted: trust.

She left her hotel, hailed a cab, and would be quite happily
alone for the next twenty minutes.

What made me go to a Saturday night dance in Crane
with Laura Nell Buncombe? Her company? Yes, of
course, and friends since childhood, through junior and
senior high school, and now, both home from Lubbock
for the summer. Boredom? No, not at home. Whatever it
was—Fate was the easy answer—she met Ralph Moeckle at the dance. And what was *he* doing there?

Why, he couldn't dance a step! At twenty-five, and six years
older, he was an attorney in his father's land office—this I learned
from his friends in Crane, not from him. Not as handsome as
Tommy Crouch nor as tall as Billy Earle Jones, Ralph had a
quiet—and to some, disquieting—way of asserting himself. "No,
I don't dance. Sorry. I have no sense of rhythm. We can walk,
though."

First and only time I'd ever heard that pitch, she remembered.

Best damned thing that ever happened to me. And Laura Nell
asking: "What did you do? How did you do it? I've had my eyes
on that boy since high school."

We walked, I said, that's all. He's solid, I told Laura Nell, and
I'm going to marry him. It wasn't until a month later that I learned
he was a Lutheran, like me. And a month after that, he had bought
the engagement ring at Reynolds'—before he asked me. He
couldn't tell a joke to save his soul from the gates of Hell, but he
enjoyed them. What he was, was a reader, and when the twins
came, he'd read to them at eight months of age. A riot.

And the twins inherited his teeth, thank God. . .

"Driver, I'll get off here and walk. Here's ten dollars for your trouble."

"But, lady, that's too much."

I too like to walk, she said to herself.

She walked into a drug store, bought a pack of cigarettes, and called Joe Eubanks on her cell phone.

"Half an hour? Good, see you then, Traudi."

●

The Southern System: Jarvis, Bonham, and Belken. Jarvis was her district, but Belken was her pet. Three years on the job, and she looked forward to her three-day stay twice a year. It would be different now with the Presidential Search; the Valley, the border, still one more distinct part of Texas. East Texas, the Caprock, her West Texas, Central Texas, and the Valley. Little Belken State, she laughed.

She had also laughed when she realized it wasn't a Valley at all; a delta, sure, but no valley. She had laughed longer when she learned that the developers named it during the boom of the twenties, and now the Mexican nationals called it El Valle and were as proud—smug, almost—of its isolation and its border culture. Well, she liked it, too. It was, to use that abused word, unique. She came to North Texas Avenue, turned east, and entered the Eubanks-Domínguez Building.

Joe Eubanks waited for his friend and colleague, friend and fellow Regent, but first, friend. Tired of Austin's meddling, he had considered resignation, but Traudi, God bless her, prevailed. "Can't let the crazies run our insane asylum."

A warm greeting, and "How is Carmelita, Joe?" The smile and answer, "Handsome as ever, Traudi, and thank you."

The applications would be coming in within three days to meet the deadline. The voters had no idea how tough a job the presidency was. The ambitious didn't care, this was their dream. The hard-bitten would make the stronger presentations, but bring no questions to the table regarding student body projections, pro-

grammatic needs and changes, new construction, needed reconstruction, would tuition go up, did it need to, a consideration of
the region's economy, and so on and on. The nuts and bolts. The
System was the System: an equal share for all on a per student
capita basis, but the Presidential Search at Belken State was the
meeting's priority, and one would judge the Faculty's recommen-
dations. The other two System presidents would be called on for
information. They would also call the president of Wilton-Fair
University for his ideas, views, opinions.

Anything that would help in the selection. He'd brought peace
and stability to a college in Oklahoma and had done the same at
Wilton. This and more was under consideration.

Would Lalo Guerra and Pete Morales push for a Mexican
American candidate? Only if the candidate were a serious con-
tender. Belken State had always fought an uphill battle, had borne
the insults, Enchiladaville, Chalupa U, etc., but the faculty had
fought back, the deans had backed them, and the tenured, attenu-
ated political hacks among them were aging. The Deans' Agreement, hashed out by them alone, to give a 3- or 4-percent raise to
everyone, worked because meaningful merit raises would come
for merit, academic contributions, and, what always mattered,
strong programs.

The Southern System was an open admissions institution, but
the students' entry scores had risen little by little, year after year.

●

"We're no UT, you all."
"That's right, but they're not Harvard either."
"They don't need to be."
"And neither do we."

●

The American Library Association gave the System its affir-
mative vote consistently, and the three university library budgets
were increased accordingly. Thanks to Nick Crowder's efforts, the

alumni base at Belken State was stronger. Yes, the other two System presidents would be called on for information.

The Southern System of State Universities was sufficient unto itself: first-generation students in West Texas and Far West Texas along with Belken by the Gulf were the "first fruits," but there were also second- and third-generation college students whose families revelled in their independence.

The search would go on. Questions were to be drawn at home, the Regents and its director, and from the area campuses, but also from alums living outside of the state. Out-of-staters were something new for a state whose regents did not stand for election but were appointed by the Governor.

Joe Eubanks had fought for some outsiders while Drew Fairbanks was for maintaining that old myth—Texas for Texans—and Drew was considered the Governor's friend. And they would vote, Joe insisted. We need their ideas on this. And Drew had stalled, demured, finally outmaneuvered, and the out-of-staters came aboard.

What mattered was the System and Belken State, and the Valley was the State's fifth most populated area: it mattered politically. Old-time friendships, time-servers, and the smilers with a knife had been running the System for too long. This System's Board would stick together. After all the discussions, they would agree, they would play no favorites. Belken State and the System mattered.

After the salad, Joe Eubanks drove Traudi to the hotel.

"They'll be in tonight, Traudi. I'll come by at seven tomorrow morning."

"Bye, dear."

First she removed her shoes and then sank into the king-sized bed fully clothed. A tiring day, but the last candidate had been interviewed. An hour later, awake and refreshed, she soaked in a warm tub for half an hour. The trial had started that morning; she glanced at her watch: six o'clock with dinner at eight. She called the Belken County Courthouse and asked for Chief Inspector Buenrostro. (Is that how his name is pronounced? I should have asked, the way he did).

"Homicide, Cantú."

"Good evening, may I speak with the Chief Inspector?"

"May I have your name, please?"

A few seconds later, Rafe Buenrostro came on the line. "Good evening, Mrs. Moeckle."

"Good evening, Chief. Any news for me?"

"Yes." The voice sounded tired; as busy as us, she thought, but easily more trying.

"You won't have to testify. The murderer confessed before the judge. His lawyers objected, and the accused fired them on the spot. When Junior Rawlings, a lawyer, tried to grab him, he was knocked down against the wall, and then all hell broke loose. It took three bailiffs to hold the accused until the judge brought the courtroom to order."

"Goodness."

"Judge Stillwell asked the accused, his name is Enos Gottschalk, Mrs. Moeckle, if he would be seeking a new attorney to represent him.

"Gottschalk said he wanted to plead guilty, period. Short, Nasty, and Brutish. . ."

"Pardon me?"

"His attorneys, Rawlings, Cortez, and Rawlings Junior, withdrew, the judge dismissed them, and they marched out of the courtroom. They're excellent attorneys, Mrs. Moeckle. They'll fight for their client as defense attorneys should."

"And?"

"The Executive D.A., Gwen Phillips, asked the judge to explain to Mr. Gottschalk that he had to allocute. This was explained to him, and he gave an account of the murder."

"It was brutal, and that's all I will say."

A relieved Traudi Moeckle said, "Thank you."

"Judge Stillwell pronounced him guilty and remanded Gottschalk into custody for sentencing next Monday."

"And that was it?"

"No. Gwen Phillips told me she had requested ninety-nine years and with no provision for parole."

"Thank God."

"Yes, he's vicious and he has no business in the streets."

"Can he recant?"

"After the allocution? No. He can try, but with twenty to thirty witnesses, he can't claim he was threatened by anyone."

A long, audible sigh. "Chief Inspector, I want to thank you for the quick resolution of this horrible crime."

"Ah, we found additional evidence, Mrs. Moeckle."

"Anything else, Mr. Buenrostro?"

"No, that's it."

"Again, thank you very much and good night."

"Good night."

Traudi Moeckle began to cry as soon as she laid down the phone. Looking at the mirror, she said, "Oh, I look such a mess," and began to dress for dinner. She called the bar for a gin and tonic and finished dressing by the time the drink arrived. She signed a healthy tip, took too big a drink, and began to choke.

"I ought to know better," she said, chiding herself.

●

At seven o'clock, Rafe Buenrostro called home.

"Hello, Chief. How are you?"

"Beat, not hungry either."

"How about I fix you a nice warm bath; it'll be waiting for you."

"I love you."

"I know that. Hurry home."

The heat and humidity in Houston are unforgiving for eight months of the year. The other four, November through February, are passable, but only that. Zoning is an unknown word there. With an occasional hurricane always a threat, and with ten-inch rains not uncommon, the streets can run like rivers.

A saving grace: by five o'clock or so, downtown Houston closes up and everybody, except for the homeless, rushes off to join clogged freeways out of town and drive to crowded suburbs. Not, then, a model for city planning, but build we must and build we will. But it's a big-league city, culturally too, and with enough recreation areas to satisfy everyone.

Sam Houston was lucky to have this hustling, bustling, energy-filled city named after him. He has not been treated well by Texans; no, not after he wisely counseled against secession. Went against the grain by heeding his father's advice and the proverb "Compliance wins friends, truth, hatred."

Statues? One, a monstrosity one can see and marvel as one drives from Houston to Huntsville. Some 120 feet high and the mass of white hair at the nape reminds one of the late Governor John Connally. Huntsville, Texas, the city of homes and churches and prisons, for criminals and civil servants alike. Sam Houston State University stands in Huntsville, a bone to some East Texans who believed in their heart of hearts, and in the heart and hearts of their parents, that Texas A&M University was too liberal.

"S.H.S.U., my alma mater," said Pete Morales. Firstborn child of foreign-born parents, Pete Morales first worked for Glen McCarthy's oil drillers as a roustabout moving from dry field to dry field until they hit a strike. He then made tool pusher and earned good money. But this was not for him. He wanted to work for himself. He had the tools—hard work and desire—but he

needed the language, which was missing at home. His father, Cre-
cencio Morales, worked for a while as an able-bodied seaman,
then as a cook for Lykes Lines. From that, a cook for the Katy
Railroad before retiring well before Social Security was enabled.
Fit at fifty, he bought a small house in Houston's tough Naviga-
tion District. He became a welder and he and his wife raised a
family of nine; two were taken by polio and the two oldest boys
by World War II. Pete, the youngest, quit high school in the tenth
grade to work with his father and to work on his G.E.D, a high
school diploma equivalent, but what equivalent meant didn't matter to him. It was a high school diploma.

Twenty-five years later, at age thirty-four, he sat in his office
of Morales Insurance and Real Estate. Hard work, of course, but
luck, too. Luck came in the form of an old oil field worker named
Hogan Scroggins, a West Texan from Wink, Morales' one and
only boss.

●

"So you're leaving, Petey? Good, you came to me as a
sixteen-year-old and you're leaving as a man of twenty-one. College, is it? Well, you're in luck. And, you're in for a surprise, too.
I deducted a dollar from your weekly paycheck when you came
to work here; there were leap years there, so you can figure out
how much you got coming to you. And how much have you
saved?"

"I've got close to nine thousand, Mr. Scroggins."

"And my savings for you comes, let's see, $2,190. That's with
interest. And that's what I call a grub stake. Still planning to go to
college? UT in Austin? They've got solid geology programs there
and petroleum engineering. Right?"

"Going to S.H.S.U. to study business. I want to work for
myself. Besides, I can always bum a ride to Houston and see my
folks once in a while."

"Not going to buy a car?"

"No, sir. I plan to work and save my money. Been sending part of my pay to my folks, but you know that. I know my dad, and I'm sure he's saved some for me."

"Never met him, would have liked to and would have thanked him. Mexican-born, was he?"

"In Juchipila, Zacatecas, a silver town, but he said enough of his people had died in the mines, and that wasn't for him."

"Winona and I are going to miss you, Petey."

"Thanks, Boss."

"You know, I never knew of a man who had two sets of parents. Old Pete Land trained you, and you only eighteen, taking to that work like it was nothing. Best tool pusher there was and then you took over. Couldn't have two Petes around the rig, so you became Petey. That mean anything in Spanish, the word *petey*?"

"Not that I'm aware."

"Old Pete lives in Menard now. Know where that is?"

And Hogan Scroggins laughed.

"I was a fool back then, Boss. I let that Neck get to me: Some jail they got in Menard. No paperwork, though, so I don't have a record."

And Pete Morales laughed.

"Right, but it cost you thirty-five hard-earned dollars out of your next paycheck. Winona was angry at me for two whole days, but you didn't lose your temper again over some damn fool riding you like that. I have to admit, I liked the way you stood up to that big, fat, beer-bellied, West Texas son-of-a-bitch. And with his friends looking on, too."

"Nothing to be proud of, though."

"No, and don't you forget it. Working in the fields ain't like living and working with so-called civilized people."

He then asked if Pete had football in mind. And Pete had shaken his head. Too hungry for football; school and work, nothing else.

"No girl?"

"That'd be a bonus. Gotta go, Boss."

"Well, if that's your last word, let's get out of here, Pete Morales. Here, give me one of those *abrazos* of yours. Careful you don't break my rib cage."

Hogan Scroggins walked him to the door and carried one of the two bags.

"What's this, lunch?"

"The deductions, take care of it, Petey."

Pete Morales shook the old man's hand.

"That Greyhound should be pulling in about now. I'm not much of a writer, but you write, you hear?"

●

"A call from President Crowder, sir."

"Thank you, Maggie. Hello, Nick. Good to hear from you."

"Pete, we're faxing the Search Committee's first write-up for you. Any changes are up to you and the Board. I just talked to Traudi, she sends her regards. I'll be calling the other Board members in a few minutes."

"Thanks for calling, Nick. Heard anything from Austin regarding our budget?"

"Yes. Got a call from Dub Bailey . . ."

"From Lockhart, right?"

"Right. Says we're doing well so far. The Governor's office hasn't said a word, though."

"Typical. Any trouble with the Coordinating Board on those new courses you all requested down there?"

"Not so far, no. I'll let you know."

"Any trouble from that front, I'll lean on 'em. Look, Houston's the only university with a similar program, and you all are over four hundred miles away, so I see no trouble with that new man they just hired."

"You know him, Pete?"

"No, but we will, I'm sure."

"Gotta run. . . and thanks, Pete."

"I'll get into Klail between one and two. See you in Lalo's office."

"Take care on the road, Pete."

A fter the table was cleared, the chairs rearranged, and the dishes carted away, Bruce Kyle moved toward the head of the table. There was no need to call the meeting to order; after the last three days, each one dedicated to the last three candidates, the Regents, tired but game, sat waiting for the wrap up which would lead to the offer of the post of president.

If the first candidate bowed out for whatever reason, they would move on to the second and, if necessary, to the third.

The three candidates' dossiers lay to Kyle's right. He turned to Drew Fairbanks who, as Director of the Board, would ask for the final assessment.

Merle Malone, Vice President for Academic Affairs at St. Christine's University was up for discussion. Her résumé and the letters of recommendation and evaluation were even with the two remaining candidates.

At mid-morning, Iain Cameron "Wild Bill" McVicar had been disposed of kindly. Drew Fairbanks had invited him to coffee.

"Looking for a younger person, Iain, not age discrimination, but the job now calls for twelve-to-fourteen-hour days. Austin has never been generous, and you've known this for the last twenty years, but this is the limit; we may just have to dip into our reserves and come up with additional money; we'll also have to depend on the generosity of the alums."

McVicar listened closely and nodded as if in agreement, an old habit.

Fairbanks' voice, decisive as always, motored on, and he smiled at the old acquaintance. McVicar took it calmly enough and yes, he would do what he could. The Board could count on him at any time.

"One question: has the candidate been chosen?"

"No, not yet. We're going into the last phase, but I wanted to see you regarding funding. I've spoken to the Governor personally any number of times, but no soap. We need you, Iain. It's been a hard year, and we're counting on you to help the incoming president. You're an old warrior, and whoever comes in will need to know the history of the place. Can you name someone who knows its history better than you?"

McVicar shook his head.

"One last favor, and it's a big one: the weatherman has predicted clear skies for the next four days. Commencement will be worry free, and the fireworks display, as always, pleases the crowd. I want you, old friend, to lead the singing of 'My Alma Mater, Tis of Thee,' to close the ceremony.

"But, before I do, I will introduce you and then present you to the audience with your new title."

McVicar seemed to have woken up.

"New title?"

"You will be introduced as the Chief Executive Officer."

"Drew."

"It's neither a favor nor a bone, Iain. You've always been faithful to Belken, and this Board knows how hard you've worked through the years."

"I, I don't know what to say."

"There's nothing to say, you've earned it. Sorry to cut the coffee short, but I've got to get upstairs and see what those people are up to."

His shoulders straightened, almost military-like. Iain Cameron McVicar extended his right hand to Fairbanks.

"Thanks, old friend."

With that chore out of the way, Fairbanks took the elevator to the Deans' room. "How did it go, Drew?"

Fairbanks looked at Mim Stockwell Burton, one of the three out-of-state regents, and pursing his lips said, "It was sad. He's an old warhorse, Mim, but I thought it best if I were the one to let him down. He sounded genuinely pleased with the new title and sends his thanks."

Fairbanks breathed rather noisily. "Are we ready for one last go-round?"

"Well, Bruce, who do we call first?"

Bruce Kyle opened the envelope marked Number One.

"Dr. Merle Malone."

"Thank you. Since the item, by state law, is a personnel matter, Bruce, I will ask you to step outside."

Lalo Guerra spoke first. "Briefly, I think we have the best candidates, and I'm happy—as I think we all are—with each one of the top three. Dr. Malone is assertive rather than aggressive. When she walked into the room and looked all around, her 'Good morning' sounded relaxed, relaxed in what is not a relaxing situation."

Murmurs of hear, hear, followed Guerra's first remarks."

"She's worked with all socioeconomic classes at St. Christine's, and she'll have more money here due to a lower tuition. Her ideas on university-wide honors programs and classes are sound: we begin with volunteers among existing professors, and an innovative push for team-teaching, long a dream here, has always had backing from the professors themselves. As we all know, the snag has always been teaching-load credits. She was the only one to offer ideas, workable ideas, on this. She's been working with the Rockefeller Foundation, the National Endowment for the Humanities, and the College Board, always a source of innovative programs. As a traditionally minority institution, I feel confident she can present a strong argument for B.S.U. regarding independent funding."

Thomas Owen Wilson, another of the out-of-state regents, said, "Don't forget NASA. She's a biophysicist, and they always call on her. This further attests her various talents."

Max Jacobs added, "She's a known quantity, and the faculty at Physical Sciences will pass the word."

"Imaginative, too."

Everyone looked at Traudi Moeckle. "Dr. Malone wants the System to be cohesive. Visiting professors between the three universities. They trade houses for a semester or for a year. We could pay for the move to and from. That won't cost much. I think it's a fine idea."

Lalo Guerra continued. "I accept that someone expressed reservations because she is single. There's always the fear of talk. . . yes, she's a former nun, and she's now forty-nine years old. What she does with her life will reflect on the university, and we do have to think of the community."

"Excuse me, Lalo."

"Traudi."

"You think she's lesbian?"

"No, and I don't care if she were or is. Some of our constituency might, but, since she isn't, there's no worry."

Traudi Moeckle cut in. "But you're worried. I mean, for the institution."

"No. I bring this up because I voted for her from the start."

Mim Stockwell: "You're not saying you had her investigated, I hope."

Guerra shook his head. "Nothing of the kind. No. I just have the gut feeling that she will do well by us. That Belken will grow and improve because of her. I brought possible rumors up, but, dammit all, I'm sick and tired of being called Taco Tech and listening to every possible denigrating name for us. To hell with that crowd."

Fairbanks looked around. "Tom? Max? Jack? You, Pete?"

Pete Morales pushed his chair back. "How about you, Drew? How do you feel?"

"She's a winner. Knowing the other two presidents in the System, she'd fit in. Pete, we've all been appointed by our respective governors, but the presidential election is a board decision. In short, we make the decisions, not the Governor. I'm for her, Pete. Let's break for dinner. Seven sharp at the Klail Arms. My thanks to everyone."

Drew Fairbanks rose at six o'clock, as always, and after his routine of the shave and the shower, he pulled on his boxer shorts and T-shirt. He then called room service: bran, no-fat milk, orange juice, a carafe of coffee, and an apple.

A man of routine, set in his ways, and to save time, he selected the suit, tie, shirt, and shoes he was to wear that morning and laid them on the bed. He discovered he had run out of handkerchiefs and made a mental note to buy half a dozen at the university bookstore.

Fifteen minutes later, a knock on the door. Ah, breakfast. Before he answered the door, he drew five dollars from his billfold and had them in hand when the breakfast trolley was rolled in. "Here's the paper, Mr. Fairbanks, and good morning to you."

"Morning, Charlie."

"Thank you, sir."

•

Phone calls, and he checked his watch. Seven-fifteen. The Governor would be up by now, and he too would be on the phone calling around the state. Fairbanks thought on this for the briefest of moments. "I'll call him at eight-thirty."

He called the desk and requested a taxi. "Fifteen minutes, sir?"

"Yes, that's fine, thanks."

He began to tick off the phone calls: his wife, the Governor, and Vice President Robert Rhodes. "Morning, Bob, Drew Fairbanks."

"Good morning. I'll have Shirley make us some coffee."

"Good. What time does the bookstore open?"

"Eight-thirty. Need something?"

"I'll drop by after we have our coffee. Need to buy some stuff for the grandkids."

"Coffee'll be here."

•

The Governor. I'll call him from Nick's office. He won't like our choice. This thought brought a smile to Drew Fairbanks' creased East Texas face.

But Fairbanks, considered the Governor's man, considered, by the uninformed, to be in the Governor's pocket, was loyal to the Southern State University System; the System was as independent as he was. Now in his third year as Director of the Board, he could see what the Governor and his hangers-on couldn't: the Valley school would follow in the footsteps of Leo Flores, the first and only Hispanic president, followed by Nick Crowder, both innovators and men of integrity. Well, and he smiled as he thought, "Well, Mr. Governor, a woman president, single, Catholic, and solid."

Fairbanks, a rancher, banker, and president of his insurance firm, loved horses and horse racing. Choosing a president was much like a horse race: the one to bet on looked good, but was it the right horse? Telephone calls all week had assured him of Merle Malone: the real goods. He looked at his notepad: calls to make to Pete Morales and to Lalo. He wrote Bruce Kyle's name and drew an asterisk.

•

Vice President Rhodes' office was a mahogany-filled office, left there by a free-spending former vice president who blew fifteen thousand dollars on the furniture and then blew out of town with an eighteen-year Mexican girl in tow. Zeke Brabham. Fifteen years since, and his name was not forgotten.

"Coffee, no sugar, right?"

"Can't teach this old dog new tricks, Bob."

"Here let's go into the Deans' Room." He pressed a button on the intercom. "No calls, Shirley, thank you."

•

Twenty minutes later, the Vice President had been informed on the candidate, who Fairbanks and the Board were convinced would take the job.

"You never were interested in the job, were you, Bob?"

"It's not something I could do well. Anything else I can do for you, Drew?"

"No. You two will make a good team. I'll drop in on Nick later this afternoon."

"Be sure and call first. Ask for Sister John Berchmann."

"As serious as that?" A sad Drew Fairbanks shook his head. Checking his watch, he said, "Need to make a call, Bob."

They shook hands and Fairbanks sat alone in the Deans' Room.

He dialed the area code to Austin. A deep, almost gruff voice answered the phone. "The Guvnor's office."

"Morning, Sam. Is the Governor up and about?"

"Yessir, Mr. Fairbanks, he's expecting your call. I'll go get him."

The Governor, and he was not alone, had not been to the Valley and neither had the previous four—five, was it?

Presently, Governor Watling Stonecutter came on. "Howdy, Drew."

"Morning, Governor. How's Austin?"

"Warmish, humid, and the usual botheration."

"Nothing you can't handle."

A flattered Governor smiled. "How about General Ordway? Any news on that front?"

Fairbanks was ready for that one. "Didn't make the cut, Watty."

"Damn! He's a good man, Drew. They need some discipline down there."

Money and other resources are what Belken and the System need, not some uniform used to giving orders. The General did not interview well. He saw the campus as something that was slow moving. Slow as molasses, as he had allowed. It was the bureaucracy, he was sure of it. Well, discipline and order were called for and he promised the Board he would start there. As for the academics of it, he would rely on his Vice President and Deans.

That was the gist of that interview. Drew Fairbanks shuddered at the thought of handing over the presidency to someone who knew nothing of university life: professors who spoke their minds, deans who backed them up if the professors were in the right, and a stalwart like Bob Rhodes judging and acting, not in haste, but after consultation. This took time, but it also prevented mistakes. Mistakes which would prove costly in morale, an important and essential element in keeping order on a campus. Order and discipline—well, he, Drew Fairbanks, had had three years of that in the army. Well and good, but a campus is not a military camp.

The Governor was not being lectured to, but he also knew when to cut his losses. Fine, General Ordway would make a good aide to the Governor, and it would look good to the bulk of the population.

"You tried your best, Drew, and I'm much obliged. Anything else?"

"Yessir. We're holding our last interview today, and we've pretty much made up our minds already. Her name is Merle Malone. She's been a chair, a dean, an associate dean in administration, and lately, St. Christine's Vice President for Academic Affairs. Assured, diplomatic, and a successful fund-raiser."

"A woman president, that's good. And Catholic. That's good, too. Have her call me when she accepts. I'd like to extend my congratulations."

"That's mighty kind of you, Watty. I'm sure she'd appreciate it."

"Anytime, Drew, boy. See you."

"Yes, good-bye."

•

A woman and a Catholic. Hmph. Wonder what the wonder-boy has planned for the General? Some sinecure, and he'll be in uniform, too. And now for the bookstore.

He telephoned Bruce Kyle.

"Bruce, Drew Fairbanks. Have someone pick up Ms. Malone at the Palm Gardens, would you?

"You'll pick her up? Good, and thank you, Bruce." He pushed the telephone away and drew out his notepad. Call to Pete M. . . but first, the bookstore. He left through the Deans' Room private entrance. On his way to the bookstore, he crossed the mall, noticed the trim gardening, and approved.

Drew Fairbanks drove into the reserved parking lot of the Lalo Guerra Enterprises building on South Blanchard in downtown Klail City. Lalo had moved to nominate Merle Malone's candidacy and Pete Morales had seconded the motion. Traudi Moeckle asked to amend the motion by adding that Dr. Malone be the first to be offered the post of president when the top three had been selected.

If, for whatever reason, she changed her mind, if, say, St. Christine's, as a private institution, offered more money, then the next candidate, Roger Velásquez would be offered the post. The third candidate, George Eustis, would follow if Velásquez stepped down. As agreed, the Board would be happy with any one of the three.

Fairbanks walked into the front office as a smiling Lalo Guerra waited for him. The two exchanged friendly greetings and Guerra led Fairbanks into his office.

On the way, Fairbanks said, "Talked to the Governor half an hour ago."

"Ah. How'd he take the non-nomination of General Brass Ass?"

Drew Fairbanks smiled. "Like a trouper."

"I'll bet," said a laughing Lalo Guerra. "Are you ready for breakfast?"

"I've eaten, thanks. I'll take a cup, though."

"Good. Pete should be here any minute now. He heard from Leo Flores late last night."

"Oh?"

"Leo said we made a fine choice, and he sends his warm regards."

"Doing all right, I imagine."

"Fighting the good fight, you know Leo."

Pete Morales strode through the main hall and stopped at the desk.

The receptionist looked up and recognized him immediately. "Good morning, sir. You know the way?"

"Blindfolded, Miss Ransom, thank you."

●

Business. They focused on Mim Burton neé Stockwell, the newest of the three recent appointments. An out-of-stater now, but Texas-born and a baccalaureate holder from Jarvis University, she had been fully expected to participate in the nomination and selection process and she had done so.

There was neither intelligence nor mention on the late Chauncey Burton, but he had left Mim and their two daughters solid, conservative investments when he disappeared after an oil exploration trip to Borneo. The plane wreckage was found seven days after the last transmission and native trackers were paid good money to find him and his pilot, an Australian named John Sharpe. To no avail.

The provident Mr. Burton had also left his survivors a half-million-dollar insurance policy, not collectible for seven years but this was nothing to Mim and their daughters. There was no need to sell any of their property; their college tuitions and expenses had been seen to years before, and the seven years passed not in relative comfort, but in quiet comfort and style.

When the Southern System convinced the previous governor that new, outside blood, albeit Texan blood, was needed, he listened carefully, asked a few questions, made numerous phone calls, and Mim Burton passed the test.

She had listened carefully and made cogent, coherent remarks that attested to her high intelligence and interest. She, alone, would not accept expenses travelling from Chicago to the meetings, wherever held. A matter of choice, she said without a scrap of officiousness; it was her way, Mim's way. Whatever the Klail City National Bank covered as their expenses for the three-day meetings, Mim Burton would write a check to the host institution to form part of the university's general scholarship fund.

A daughter finished at Rollins and earned a degree in theatre design at NYU; the youngest, Marjorie, had been accepted at the Parish School of Design. Very middle-class outlook in many ways, but the money and the class showed through. Flaunting had been frowned upon since childhood, and their father, a take-no-prisoners investment banker from Chicago, led a blameless life except for the profitable forays he would make, from time to time, into the world of New York finance. A Midwesterner and proud of it, he was also proud of his Welsh background. As his mother, a Pembroke, used to say, the Welsh were people who prayed on their knees and preyed on their neighbors.

To be mourned by Mim and kept in their daughter's memory as a warm, loving father attested Chauncey Burton's productive fifty-five years of life on earth.

Mim gladly accepted the opportunity to serve her alma mater and the two other campuses in the System. Serious but not solemn, she had not lost that West Texas drawl nor the humor that comes from a region which Hollywood shows as cattle country, while its natives know that the country is more fit for goats than for cattle. Profitable Mohair goats, to be sure, but goats they are, and not cattle.

And she would make the formal offer to Merle Malone.

D rew Fairbanks rose from the dinner table at the Klail Arms' private banquet room and smiled.

There, thought Pete Morales, is a happy man. I'll have to reassess my opinion of Mr. Drew Fairbanks.

Fairbanks raised a glass of ice water and said, "As a master's degree holder of Alanon, I toast and congratulate all of us. I also want to thank Max Jacobs for his note-taking."

"Hear, hear."

"I also want to thank Lalo for setting a record for the least number of interruptions in the three years we've worked together. Lalo."

Lalo Guerra, the one Klail native on the Board, rose and raised his glass of Medoc in recognition. "Mim, I thank you for your thoughtful remarks and for accepting membership on the Board. It's a wrench, and your first meeting was a most important one for the System and for Belken State.

"None of us is a graduate of Belken, but we serve, as you have during this session, with spirit. We also have a small present for you."

"Oh, no," said a surprised Miriam Stockwell.

"Joe, walk on over and remember to keep it short."

A smiling Joe Eubanks said, "For you, Mim, with our best wishes."

"Oh, it's lovely, but what is it?"

Pete Morales said, "*Una mantilla de Manila.*"

"I do have to brush up on my Spanish. What did you say, Pete?"

He looked at the delicately woven, black and silver shawl and said, "Made in Manila, by hand. You'll be the envy of everyone in Chicago."

"It's gorgeous."

"Put it on. Traudi, help her out." This from Joe Eubanks as he led the applause.

Fairbanks stood up again. "Pete, a brief prayer of thanks for Nick."

●

After another fifteen minutes of socializing, Fairbanks said, "If you look in the coming agenda, our next meeting will be held in Jacksboro in three months. I'll call Dean Brothers after we break up, and I'll ask about Nick's condition.

"Night, night, everybody, and thanks, once again."

●

"Oh, Pete."

"Yes, Traudi."

"Drew says you're a hunter. We've got some fine white tails in West Texas. They dress out at ninety to one hundred pounds."

"Well, thank you, Traudi. I'll give you plenty of warning before I head on out there."

●

Max Jacobs walked out with Joe Eubanks.

"Heard anything about Nick?"

"The end is quite near. I talked to the head nurse before coming here."

"Tonight, you think?"

"Could be, could be tomorrow, tonight. He's in deep pain now"

"Were the flowers delivered today?"

"Yes, Susie called to thank us. You can imagine the overflow; at Susie's request, many have been passed on to some of the other patients."

Max Jacobs shook his head slowly. "Too bad. Nick was a fine, first-class man. I think we should stick around until tomorrow afternoon. You never can tell."

"I'll talk to Drew and have him leave messages all around. It's a fine suggestion, Max. Good night."

"Good night."

It had been a long day: a long day on the phone with the Governor, the meeting with Lalo and Pete, the assigning of Mim Stockwell to present the offer to Merle Malone, the worrying over the coming loss of a dear friend, and he needed a drink. As Drew Fairbanks had said, on numerous occasions, that he had earned a master's degree in liquor, he had steadfastly (and, as he recognized, with his wife's unnagging help) abstained through business meetings and luncheons, through boredom, cocktail parties, and such. He had held a glass of ice water and thought on his twenty-two years, to the day, he reminded himself, when he resolved to stop drinking all manner of alcohol; and that also meant the suppression of beer, his one love at Duke. But now at the Klail Arms, he was tired, and he did need a drink.

It was too much, and he picked up the phone.

•

In Austin, twenty years ago, Drew Fairbanks—firstborn of an old East Texas family who didn't use that term but rather Eastern Texas, as the old settlers had—was stopped by a state trooper not far from the State capitol building. He was, in a word, drunk and driving while under the influence. Fairbanks had stopped for a red light and had then passed out. Not much traffic in Austin in those days, not at two o'clock in the morning, and the trooper knocked on the window. Fairbanks opened his eyes and, after the trooper motioned for him to lower the window, he did so.

The trooper recognized him. "Mr. Fairbanks, sir, I think you need some help. I'll call a friend, and he can drive you. . . are you staying at the Perry?"

Drew Fairbanks had mumbled a yesh, officer, and fell asleep again. Fifteen minutes later, another trooper drove up.

"Billy Don, please drive Mr. Fairbanks to the Perry. He's not feeling well."

Billy Don Frazier nodded. He woke Fairbanks and asked him to move to the passenger's side. The motor was still running and trooper Frazier drove him to his hotel.

There had been no written report, and the event went unreported.

The next morning, dressed still in his tuxedo, shoes on, and with another hacking hangover, Fairbanks called his wife.

"It's me, Drew." He went on to explain that he was still in his tuxedo, had his shoes on, and had no idea how he got to his hotel room.

"I don't think I drove. Come to that, I don't remember anything after I left the election party."

Pamela Fairbanks listened; it was a familiar story. Solicitous as ever, she said, "Stay in bed, dear. I'll take a plane and be there before noon."

●

Not one word of reproach and that had been twenty-two years ago. His drinking was treated as an illness, he underwent countless therapy sessions, and finally A.A. That did it.

●

He had always been a sound lawyer when sober, and this, too, was much of the time. But when offered a drink, he had also been unable to resist. Willpower and friends would see him through, and they did. His taste for food returned, he then quit smoking, and the taste improved.

But now, alone, after a hard day's work and after the thousands of nights when he wanted a drink and had fought the urge, the drive for just one bourbon and branch water, that damned disease, he began to weaken. He looked at the phone and returned it to the cradle. No, dammit, I won't.

He undressed slowly, thinking back on the black years, as he called them. He slipped into his pajamas, prayed, and unplugged the phone next to his bed. After all of these years, he thought. After all of these years, he repeated. The past few days had been too much and now Nick Crowder was dying at Mercy Hospital.

Drew Fairbanks rose and fumbled for the telephone connection.

He dialed home and Pamela answered the phone.

"Pam, it's about Nick Crowder, it's worse than we thought. He won't last much longer, perhaps this weekend, I don't know."

Pamela Fairbanks said, "Do you want a drink, Drew?"

"I did, but I fought it."

"I'll order flowers and take the earliest flight to Klail."

She then asked if some of the regents would stay in Klail. If so, she would also pack a black outfit."

"I'm proud of you."

Drew Fairbanks smiled. "I love you, too."

# THE BANKERS
# V

Seventy-eight-year-old Noddy Perkins, Board Chairman of the Klail City National Bank, walked into his bank with his usual sprightly step. A smile here, a good morning there, and a wave over there, got him to his office.

Connie Olvera, his longtime secretary, stepped in: coffee, black, and set it on the end table.

"Morning, Mr. Perkins."

"Good morning, Connie."

She acknowledged the greeting but her eyes were fixed on a five-foot long photograph in black and white on the wall behind Perkins' desk. The faces were remarkably clear for such a large photo.

"What're you looking at, Connie?"

"That picture, the photograph. The people look kinda funny. I remember it disappeared one day and it was back in a month or so, nicely reconstructed frame and all. I've always been curious about it."

"That photo was taken by a man named Goddard from San Antonio. He specialized in those wide-angle jobs."

"It's nice. Is that the date, there, written in white?"

"It is. Below it, in handwritten print, it says KCNB Reconstruction. We had a fire here. I was a young man then."

"They lost all the money?"

Perkins smiled. "No, not a penny. The money was in the underground safe, just like the one we have now."

Connie Olvera looked surprised. "Mr. Perkins, do you know how long I've worked at the bank?"

Perkins smiled again. "Eighteen years. But why the change in subject, Connie?"

"Oh, I'm not changing the subject. I'm surprised, though. I've been here all that time, I'm your personal secretary, and I didn't know we had an underground safe. I always thought that was the safe, there, with that huge steel door and that wheel." This brought a cackle from Perkins. "Oh, that's where we keep the customers' safety deposit boxes. You press a button to your left, it's flush with the wall, and a sliding door opens up. Simple as that. You walk downstairs and there it is."

"My goodness. . . Oh, I've drawn up yesterday's accounts for you."

"Has Mr. Malacara seen them?"

"Yessir, early this morning, before we opened."

Perkins sat back and said, "Let it go. If Jehú checked them, that's it. Speaking of Mr. M., is he about?"

"No, sir. Mr. Malacara had breakfast with Mr. Marchbanks at the college."

"Fairbanks, Connie."

"Yes, sir. We, ah. . ."

Perkins smacked his lips after the least sip of his coffee. "You were saying?"

"We, ah, the Mexican community, sir, is very proud that Mr. Malacara is a bank president."

Perkins grinned and said, "Well, let's say he's earned every penny of it these last eight years."

"Me, too, sir, I'm very proud of him."

"And how is Edelmiro doing? Everything going well?"

"Oh, yessir. Thank you. I'll call you as soon as Mr. Malacara comes in."

●

"Rushing off, Jehú?"

"Yep, I've got two pieces of business to work out before lunch."

"How's Noddy?"

"Meaner'n a snake."

"Glad to hear it."

Drew Fairbanks was still laughing as Jehú rose from his chair.

"Got us a candidate, and I'll call her before noon."

"Thanks for the confidence. Hiring in-house?"

"No. A woman VP from St. Christine's."

Malacara nodded. "Good school."

"Fine candidate. Say 'hi' to Noddy for me. When are you heading back to the bank?"

"As soon as I can. Give Pam a hug for me."

"I will. She'll be here soon."

"Nick?"

Drew nodded, walked around the meeting table, and put his arm around Jehú. "You're losing a good friend, aren't you?"

"A good and close friend. See you, Drew."

●

Jehú Malacara parked his car behind the bank, rounded the corner to the newsstand, and deposited a quarter for his copy of the *Klail City Enterprise News*. He folded it, and once inside the bank, walked straight to his office. Lucille Murray motioned: Coffee? A smile and a no thanks.

That university coffee was the worst.

He sat behind his desk and shuffled through his In basket. That can wait, he said to himself.

He called Noddy Perkins. "Morning."

"Anything pressing? If not, can you come over?"

"On my way."

●

Malacara stopped by the desk of Lucille Murray's assistant. "Elia, no calls?"

"No, sir, and good morning."

"Thanks."

●

"Sit down, sit down. Did you know that Connie didn't know our safe was underground?"

"No, I didn't know she didn't know." Jehú gave a short laugh. "I can't count the times E.B. told me about it."

Perkins frowned at the mention of his deceased brother-in-law. "That man couldn't keep a confidence, let alone a secret."

"It looks like Hitler's bunker to me."

"I guess it kinda does. . . How did it go with Fairbanks?"

"Good. They've got themselves a candidate, and the Board does want her to accept."

"Her?"

Jehú went on to explain who she was. He then mentioned Mim Stockwell and briefed the old man.

"Anything else?"

"The usual. Told Drew not to worry about expenses, hotel, food, rentals, travel. The usual."

Noddy Perkins listened and nodded.

Jehú said, "I wonder once in a while if that's okay?"

"One of our top customers. You think the Governor and all those yahoos up in Austin pay for a lot of their stuff? Shoot. Anything else?"

"Closed the Jackaman estate. Mrs. Jackaman also wants us to handle the real estate."

"No, pass that on to Lalo Guerra. Next?"

"Flora's and Jonesville's Magic Malls want to add 15,000 feet, each, to make room for some departments. I gave the go ahead."

"That's a bunch of smart people they've got out there."

"Decisive, too. Anyway, that's about it right now."

"Oh, before you go. . . we'd like for you and Becky to come over for dinner next Friday."

"What time?"

That was settled, and then Perkins, smiling and with a twinkle in his old eyes, asked, "And where's Charlie going to school in September?"

"S.M.U. He says they've got a first-class television program."

"Ha, serves you right. You've been prepping that boy for Austin all his life, and here he is, going to Dallas."

"Can't win 'em all."

"I know you're the boss and all, Jehú, but call Becky and check with her."

"I'm no fool. You said so yourself when you hired me at the old savings and loan years ago."

"Get out of here and go make us some more money."

# KIT and LOUISE BROTHERS
## VI

K it Brothers parked across the street from the emergency exit of Mercy Hospital. He put on his sunglasses and walked through the Fredericka Klail parking lot. The blacktop shimmered with the heat, and he removed his seersucker suit jacket as he walked toward the main entrance. The white heat beat down the fronds of the Belle-Tru palm trees, and the empty park benches radiated heat felt by the passersby.

Summer had hit the Valley with a hard rain every third or fourth day the first three weeks of May. This was Monday, the 23rd, and the previous night's graduation exercises had gone off exceptionally well with Wild Man Bill as acting president and wearing that famous smile as Chief Executive Officer. A consolation prize, but he'd carried his part well.

Susie Crowder called, and would he stay with Nick? She was driving to the Jonesville airport to pick up Tim coming in from Fort Worth. Kit would give Nick the news: the Board had agreed on a candidate.

On the way to the elevator, Sister John Berchmann greeted him: "Dr. Crowder is waiting for you, sir."

He nodded and waited for her to enter the elevator.

"Third, please."

"And how is he, Sister?"

"He's near the end," resignedly. "Dr. Brothers, he's such a fine, strong, beautiful man."

The elevator stopped. "Good-bye, Sister." He went to the sixth floor and knocked gently as he pushed the door, which was lightly ajar.

A weak voice said, "I'm not asleep. Oh, Kit. Any news from the conclave, has the white smoke made its announcement?"

Brothers smiled at the allusion. "Bruce called me on my cell phone on my way to see you. Drew Fairbanks made the offer and she accepted."

"Good," the voice was weaker now.

"Her name is Merle Malone. The V.P. for Academic Affairs at St. Christine's. I've met her, Nick. It was at a conference in Dallas a few years ago.

A tired sigh from Nick Crowder. "And?"

"Unanimous approval."

"You?"

"Saw her vita—she's active, Nick. And Bruce was impressed. Quiet, composed, but there's a spine back there. You'd like her as a person, too. She'll do."

"I slept last night."

"Sorry?"

"No sleep in a week. This damn thing has spread, and I'm in pain. But I slept. Woke up just fine this morning."

"It's afternoon, Nick."

Crowder smiled and grimaced almost immediately. "A bonus."

He coughed lightly. This produced a pain that Kit Brothers could feel.

"I'm tired, Kit. You go on, call the Sister. I want a pill." Brothers hesitated.

"Please, Kit, go."

Brothers hesitated briefly and then said, "I'll be back."

Nick closed his eyes and said, "Good."

Kit Brothers stopped one of the young volunteers and told her to find Sister John Berchmann. "Dr. Crowder needs to see her. Please hurry."

He sent me away. I shouldn't have left, I shouldn't have let him. That's why he'd sent Susie away. Tim could have rented a car, but Nick didn't want them to see him die.

Disgusted with himself, he turned to a side street as he mur-

mured *in pace . . . dormiam,* and he recalled one of Nick's favorites: "I do not know what sweetness of the natural land alone draws us all, and does not let us be unmindful of it."

By the time he pulled into the carport, he had finished his ninth Our Father.

"Kit?"

"I'm in the kitchen, hon."

"Get the phone, will you? My hands are all wet."

"Hello, this is the Brothers' residence."

"Doctor, this is Sister John Berchmann. . . Doctor?"

"Sorry, Sister, what can I do for you?"

"He's dead, sir. I couldn't hear what he said, his last words, I mean."

"My wife and I will be right over."

"Do hurry, please. Mrs. Crowder isn't back from the airport yet."

"Thank you."

"Nick?"

"Yes. Let's go to Mercy. Susie and Tim aren't there yet. We need to get there before Susie arrives."

"Right now. I'll go like this, all I need are my shoes."

●

He went outside, got in the car, and turned on the air conditioner while he waited for Louise. In the rearview mirror, he could see a kid on a blue bike delivering the afternoon paper, kids, screaming and laughing, playing tag, a neighbor pulling into her driveway with her youngster in a baseball uniform. Another bright blue-sky day in the small university town. Life went on. And yet. . .

"Son of a bitch."

# Also by Rolando Hinojosa

*Los amigos de Becky*

*Ask a Policeman: A Rafe Buenrostro Mystery*

*Becky and Her Friends*

*Dear Rafe / Mi querido Rafa*

*Klail City*

*Rites and Witnesses*

*The Useless Servants*